power to charm

COZY STORIES ABOUT A WITCH, A COTTAGE, AND UNEXPECTED FRIENDS

CARLY STEVENS

contents

POWER TO CHARM

AUTUMN SURPRISE

HALLOWEEN SPOOKS

LOST HEDGEHOG

YULETIDE MAGIC

ROGUE SPELLS

GARDEN SWING

power to charm

CHAPTER 1

visitors

When Ophelia snuggled into her favorite plush armchair, patchy from so many mendings, she expected no visitors.

Every day for the past eight hundred and sixty-seven days had been relatively the same. She woke in a pile of comforters, shuffled out to the little kitchen, moved enough bottles and ingredients out of the way to create a space to set her tea, and lit the kitchen fire. She allowed one fragrant log per day. Something about the luscious woodsy smell energized her after breakfast to go out into the garden. She turned on the generator that powered the fairy lights—she'd started with candles, but the bees couldn't produce wax at that volume. Besides, the voice of the garden badger spoke in the back of her mind, pestering her to think of sensible solutions. (It didn't really speak, but she had invented names and personalities for all the creatures near her home.) It said, "Now, Ophelia, there's no sense in burning down your cottage. It cannot be rebuilt." To which she mentally responded, "But Polonius, my dear sir, life must be more than caution." Then she would light a candle by the big armchair every night and imagine him scowling.

Today, however, was different. There was a muffled call. A knock.

Even eight hundred and sixty-seven days ago, there had been no one outside. That date marked the anniversary of her finishing construction on the cottage. She celebrated the occasion with a flask of brandy and a few self-indulgent sparkling spells in the fireplace every six months. Why wait a year? she reasoned.

"Now who...?" she began, untangling herself from book and blankets to rise and see who was out there. Whoever they were must have been in trouble. That, or they were trouble. She imagined the hedgehog (whom she had named Daisy) becoming very nervous at this development. Daisy was always skittering away from some perceived danger or other.

Shoving her feet in fluffy slippers, Ophelia made her way through the series of small, burrow-like rooms to the garden. The perpetual half-light provided by strings of bulbs and fairy lights hanging above the paths lit her way. Some of the lights had gone out, but she either couldn't salvage replacements or didn't have the mechanical knowledge to coax them back to life. She trundled past beds of thyme, wild roses, fennel. Gertrude the gray rabbit poked her head above the pansies. She chewed one in her mouth, quickly and guiltily, like rabbits do. She should be guilty, eating all the pansies, but Ophelia didn't find it in herself to be upset. Primroses lined the path as she went further. Right in the middle of the plants and vegetables, she'd made a mushroom out of extra materials, tall as her knee. The snails loved it.

She rarely took the longest path to its end. On most days, there was no reason to. It was more pleasant to imagine that the enchanted forest on the edge of her cottage was real.

She had spent months painting the wall to resemble trees, complete with forced perspective indicating tiny, winged fairies in the distance, flitting among birches and pines. Wispy lights and wolf shadows hid wherever she fancied them. Not in nine hundred and ten days had she opened the door hidden in the painted gorse bush.

The metal knob was warm. She had to yank before it would give. The pleasant green smell of her cottage home was instantly replaced by the dusty, sharp smell of a space enclosed by metal sheeting. She wrinkled her nose and trotted the short distance between the Inner Box and the Outer Wall, where a solid, deadbolted slab of steel twice her height loomed.

Something pounded again on the outside.

"Who's there?" Ophelia called as she rummaged in her pockets for the tincture she'd made just that week to make it easier to move heavy objects. This bolted door certainly qualified. Ingredients for this kind of potion were scarce, but she'd needed to lug a boulder to the edge of the garden to make room for planting more tomatoes. Having a strong helper would have made the task much simpler, but she was able, so she did.

"Long live the King!" came the croaky response.

Ophelia rolled her eyes. She had no interest in ancient alliances from that godforsaken war. Many still sided with Hamlet's faction, which seemed foolish to her since, according to the story, he had been one of the first to die and had left no heir. What did it even mean to fight on his side? Or, for that matter, against him? Regardless, her mother had named her Ophelia IV in hopes that she would keep their cause alive.

Now, very little was alive at all.

In the absence of people and the presence of dangerous toxin when the war went too far, it wasn't a difficult choice to fight for her own happiness instead of on behalf of a new person to keep the conflict going.

"*At his head a grass-green turf,*" she whispered once she had finally discovered the tincture in a pocket. "*At his heels a stone.*"

Unstoppering the bottle, she poured out a single drop on the big deadbolt drawn across the door. Thirteen seconds later (numbers were very important) she slid it to the side easily and cracked open the portal. A sliver of too-bright light over a too-white landscape appeared through it. The air outside was cold, even though the sliding metal bolt was hot.

"In, in!" she insisted, making sure only to exhale until the door was shut.

Two male figures slipped through the tiny opening.

They were specter-thin and white as specters too. She wasn't surprised. They must have had an enormous amount of toxin in their systems. Those side-effects weren't pleasant. She knew from experience.

"Let's get you inside," she said, shooing them toward the Inner Box.

CHAPTER 2

Tea

The men shivered, eyes down, evidently too focused on their own survival to notice the oddness of their rescuer's fluffy slippers or the potion bottle which she swiftly pocketed within her robe. The visitors wore white. Old off-duty infantry uniforms, they looked like. The red stitching was coming loose, and the older one had a rip in the knee.

The men might have been father and son. The younger of the two looked around twenty and the older maybe forty-five. That would make Ophelia right between. Closer, perhaps, to the father's age. Of course, it was difficult to tell if they'd been out in the elements for long. How on earth had that happened? Were they lost vigilantes?

She dismissed the thought and ushered them inside her sanctuary. Relief covered her head to foot when the smell of fragrant smoke and flower blossoms replaced the acrid metal odor.

As if waking up, the two men blinked at her little haven.

She didn't bother hiding her smile. She was absurdly proud of the garden with all its plants and creatures and fantastical little additions. Beyond that was the cottage, misshapen and chimneyed, with a little turret and lovely shingles that she slid down into a thick patch of heather on days when she wanted excitement. The glassless windows were rimmed with shutters, now flown open.

The visitors' eyes trailed upward, following the path of the thin curl of smoke. Above the bulbs and fairy lights, glow worms oozed blue magic along the invisible ceiling.

Finally, the two looked at her.

"Tea?" she asked.

The younger man's mouth opened in astonishment. The poor thing's lips were parched, as white as the rest of his face.

"How many people live here?" asked the older. His voice was low and the rasp made it almost musical. She'd forgotten how much she loved voices.

Ignoring his feverish, ice-blue stare and instead heading back along the path to the house, she answered, "Three, now."

"All Liegemen?"

She sighed. "It sounds like two of you are."

"You're not with the Resolutes?"

She paused and spun to face them. Daisy the hedgehog chirped and turned tail at the movement. "I'm with no one. Now, do you want a cup of tea? I also have soup and scones from my supper left over."

The younger man swallowed, but the elder frowned.

"Very good, then," Ophelia said, not giving them a

chance to answer. *It's all right, Daisy*, she thought. *I don't think they're harmful. And if they are, I'll give them a reason not to come back.* She wasn't a vindictive person, far from it, but she did keep a small bottle of dreadful metal-black potion just in case.

She didn't stop until she reached the front door. "Try not to track in too much mud. It sticks terribly." Really, she didn't mind sweeping out her kitchen, but heaven only knew where these two had been in their travels. If they had brought remnants of aggressive weeds with them, she'd be cross.

She padded through the kitchen and unearthed two clay mugs. "Here," she said. "Take this and go sit down." Easing the kettle off the fire, she poured two cupsful of bramble and mint tea. Even the older man moved somewhat in a daze as she directed them to the two coziest seats in the house. They were actually some of the only seats in the house, since, again, she never had visitors.

She watched them take tentative sips, and then deeper ones, their eyes closing in ecstasy. It was nice to have confirmation that she truly did brew excellent tea. At this rate, they'd finish in seconds, so she went to brew another pot. Into this one she added a touch of a warming potion. Only then did it occur to her to ask their names.

"Marcellus," said the younger.

"Barnardo," said the older.

"Jam?" asked Ophelia. She had clotted cream too, but that was harder to make, so she kept it for herself. In fact, it had been so long since she shared anything (not counting the crumbs and veggies she occasionally shared with Polonius and the others) that excitement bordering on irritation kept her moving.

"We lost our airship," Barnardo explained to her back as she scurried to get the scones.

She plucked two from the mound she'd baked last night and set them on little flowered plates. A scoop of jam for each and she was back in the room with the others. "How unfortunate." The men took the food gratefully.

"Engine malfunction," the younger Marcellus put in. Faint oily streaks coated his hands, now that she was looking at them, and consequently got on her dishware.

Ophelia pressed her lips together. "Before you touch anything else, kindly wash your hands."

Marcellus nodded, but Barnardo peered at her curiously as if she were some fairy tale creature come to life. Well, she mused, perhaps she was, in a way.

"It was light outside," she continued brusquely. "What time is it?"

"Around three, probably," Marcellus offered, biting into the scone.

Ophelia took her clock off the wall. It was a confection of metal and gears and painted birds that she'd worked very hard on, and it irked her that it had missed the actual time by so much. "Is that the most exact number you can conjure?" she asked, letting the annoyance show that anybody would feel if they were told they had to stay awake hours longer than anticipated.

One of the little screws holding the mechanism in place fell and got lost in the fluff of one of her slippers.

Barnardo cleared his throat and glanced with pretend

casualness at his wristwatch. Ophelia's eyebrows shot up. Barnardo, and maybe Marcellus by extension, were well off.

"It is currently three fifty-three," he declared.

"That's better." She wound up her clock to read the same time. Even wristwatches were fallible, but at least her time would be more accurate now. It was no wonder that that good-dreams spell was sputtery last week. One was less likely to need good dreams at four in the afternoon.

Placing the clock (with the strong ticking seconds that she had engineered) back on the wall, she returned her attention to the two men. Some color had returned to both of their cheeks. Now they didn't look entirely like ghosts.

"Have you not been outside?" Barnardo asked, much of his earlier wariness melting into curiosity.

Marcellus stuffed the rest of the scone in his mouth.

"Of course I've been outside," Ophelia replied. "How do you think I did all this?" She paused to let them take in the crackle of the fire, the hum of bugs, the faint tinny noise of magic, and of course the ticking clock.

"You made this all yourself?" Marcellus gazed around, eyes wide, just as she hoped he would.

"That's right." Her neck heated with pride. "Wash up and then I'll show you."

The men were not going to die now after having consuming both warming tea and a jammy scone, so it was only fair that she show off her years' long project.

Projects, plural. If she separated them into the major categories of house, garden, and magic, there were roughly forty significant projects she had completed while she was alone. All this glorious comfort, exactly how she liked it, and no one to say "how beautiful, Ophelia", "isn't this lovely, Ophelia", "oh, it's like a wonderland, Ophelia."

The disruption of visitors took on a new dimension. She would make them utterly comfortable here. Because, of course, they would be staying. What other choice could there be? They'd already absorbed far too much toxin to go out into the wild again.

CHAPTER 3

remedies

She showed them the bathroom, which was just as wonderful as the cluttered kitchen or the chairs with all the knits strewn across them. A big claw-footed tub she'd fashioned from parts stood in the center of the tiled room, with leafy plants trailing down the corners. It had hot running water and scented oils and spongey scrubbers.

"You can take turns," she declared.

"You go first," said Marcellus.

Barnardo didn't argue. It seemed they had quite the day. Ophelia deposited a soft towel on a stand beside the tub, where she often set a book to read, and closed the door.

Outside the bathroom, between Marcellus and Ophelia, was a window to the garden—she liked having windows everywhere—and a bird perched in the opening.

"Birds," Marcellus said in wonder, staring at its gray and red plumage.

"In the beginning, I'd rescue every creature I could find

and bring them here. Many generations of them now. They think this is all there is."

Marcellus made a thoughtful noise and followed her back into the kitchen. They had to pass her favorite armchair, which now had a very self-satisfied hedgehog sitting in it. Daisy was so comfortable that she barely quivered before settling down again, all but smiling with enjoyment. *You're welcome,* Ophelia thought, *but you know you aren't allowed to stay there. Enjoy it while you can!*

Back in the kitchen, one of the more temperamental poisons murmured about how the garlic was too close to its bottle. Ophelia picked up the end of the garlic strand and flipped it over the string from which it hung.

"Satisfied?" she muttered under her breath. The offended bottle sparkled purple in response.

"What are you doing?" Marcellus asked, as she rummaged through the sea of clinking jars to find the one she was looking for.

"Ha!" She emerged with a jar a little bigger than most of the others. "Here it is. Close your eyes."

"What?"

"Close your eyes. This will reduce the spread of toxin in your system."

"I don't think—"

"Don't tell me you'd rather wait until your bones deteriorate. Now, do as I say."

With a befuddled expression, Marcellus finally obeyed.

"*A mote it is to trouble the mind's eye,*" she chanted. Potions liked poetry, or meter at least. Without it, concoctions acted sullen and sluggish. The purple poison was partial to the slaying of Julius Caesar. "*Sick almost to doomsday with eclipse.*" She dabbed drops on Marcellus's right eyelid, left eyelid, bottom lip, and chin. "*Heal our climature and countrymen.*"

He scrunched one eye open.

Ophelia closed the bottle and returned it to the chaos of others, near the edge so she could find it again once Barnardo emerged. "There." She dusted her hands.

"Should I feel any different?"

She bit back a smile. "No. Just thank me when you wake up tomorrow with no aches and a pleasant taste in your mouth."

He smacked his still-dry lips together. "Are you... um..."

She put her hands on her hips, daring him to continue. The poor boy looked so uncomfortable. He tapped one oil-slicked finger against his white trousers, looking everywhere but at her. He might have been younger than twenty after all. Life as an airship mechanic (which she guessed he was) wasn't an easy one. Skin was chapped raw by the toxic air, and the constant threat of death made people age more quickly. Marcellus, despite being dry and skinny and pale, had big eyes darker than the older man's. Lines around his mouth showed a ready range of emotions.

"Say it," she prompted, not unkindly.

He hesitated. Most children grew up silently. "Hold your tongue" was the common refrain, so she knew this might be hard for him, even if he was a young man now.

"Are you a witch?"

She beamed. "Of sorts. Sometimes by necessity and sometimes because I want to."

Marcellus went still.

"Oh, don't act like I'm going to enchant you into a horny toad. I already have one of those. His name is Fortinbras and I doubt he would enjoy any competition."

He burst out laughing. Fortinbras was a common name —like Ophelia, like Gertrude—but usually among the Resolutes. She cared nothing for politics, or the horrible war outside, but she suspected that detail would please both her guests.

"You're giving away our secrets," Polonius the badger would say.

"Dreadfully personal," she would respond, "the name of a horny toad."

Then he'd huff and return to his little badger armchair by the fire.

Marcellus helped her clean the dishes, helped himself to another scone, and washed up after Barnardo emerged, clean and damp.

Ophelia insisted that they not put on their dirty white uniforms after having washed, so she provided them with clothes she'd made instead. They grumbled as they took the garments, but the grumbling ceased after they felt how comfortable they were. Barnardo wore a thick blue sweater and brown trousers, both a little too short but snuggly all the same. Marcellus had on her best long robe. Tonight, she was wearing her second-best robe, and she figured it was the least she could do for two stranded crash victims who had stumbled on her place.

As promised, she gave them a tour around the cottage and grounds. They lingered a particularly long time in the turret library, where shelves and shelves of books wrapped around the circular room so high she'd had to craft a ladder out of old engine parts just to reach them. Marcellus named all the parts as if that were what she wanted to show off. Spines glittered among fairy lights—grimoires and plays, construction manuals and bawdy tales. Anything she had bought or foraged that held any interest for her was gathered here. If a book was ugly or torn, she re-bound it. Some of the spines had no title at all, just a symbol, her own kind of code. That skinny book had a mushroom on it. That thicker one had the face of a goblin. She'd enjoyed drawing that and giving herself shivers.

"It's a longitudinal girder," Marcellus exclaimed. "Ingenious! Is that part of a ballonet?" He scurried off to the opposite side of the room to run his hand over the fabric curtains framing one section of books.

Barnardo remained staring at a tiny mechanical dancer up on one delicate toe.

After a beat of too-long silence, Ophelia drew the trinket off its shelf. "It dances. See?" She wound the mechanism and the dancer twirled, tinkling music accompanying her movement.

Barnardo laughed with delight, but then his smile faded and his icy eyes grew wet. Ophelia placed the dancer back where it came from. She hadn't meant to upset him.

"My daughter dances," he explained.

"Where is she?" Ophelia asked.

Barnardo's throat moved and he slid his eyes away.

"Has that bulb gone out?"

They both looked at Marcellus, who was pointing at the ceiling.

"Yes," Ophelia answered. She'd forgotten all about that light hanging from metal piping.

"Would you like me to fix it for you?"

A funny twist in her chest mirrored on her lips. "Yes, please."

Marcellus puffed himself up, apparently smug to know that he could name all the engine parts and repair broken pieces of her cottage.

Barnardo cast Ophelia a secret look. It was like having a friend.

CHAPTER 4

resolute

M arcellus would begin small repairs tomorrow, and a fizz of anticipation roiled inside her. It was only a lightbulb, but it felt like more. Now her spines would glow brighter with their little pictures, all because a friendly stranger offered to help.

She continued the tour, showing them rooms with hanging herbs and little cauldrons, recesses with artwork filling every cranny of wall space, and even her curtained bedroom with one of the precious wax candles in it.

Barnardo's sparce comments about the construction and Marcellus's treasure hunt for engine parts became exclamations of "oh, look at that!" "There's another one!" "Come over here. You have to see this!"

Ophelia all but stopped giving the tour, instead swaying with her hands clasped behind her back, glowing with pride. Even her own family never got to see this home—she only began creating it after illness from the toxin had taken the last of them.

Marcellus and Barnardo, wrapped in her woven rabbit fur garments, pointed under a glass cloche at a stuffed Elf Owl.

"This is remarkable," Barnardo finally said, meeting her eyes.

"Yes, well. The sun may say differently, but I feel it's time for bed. It will take me a few days to adjust."

Barnardo consulted his watch with no attempt at subtlety.

"You said something about soup," Marcellus said carefully.

She grunted as she remembered her earlier promise. "There are bowls in the kitchen. Don't add anything from the bottles unless you want to wake up covered in bark with your feet growing roots. And don't listen to what they say either. The wispy red one is a terrible gossip—don't take it to heart. Leek and onion soup is in the vat near the fire. Clean up after yourselves!"

Barnardo cast a look around the cluttered space as if to comment about cleanliness, but Ophelia merely stared at him. Cluttered wasn't the same as messy. Or maybe it was.

"When you're finished, you'll stay in this room." She had created two bedrooms, for variety's sake, maybe. The second bedroom was rounded, like many of the walls, with quaint little pictures, a shelf of plants, and a mattress laden with quilts. Now, all that time spent tinkering and knitting and hanging lights in that room would pay off.

"Thank you," said Marcellus eagerly.

Barnardo sighed. His shoulders lost the rest of their stiffness. He still looked pale—the inevitable effect of being outside without enough protection—but his light blue eyes softened. They weren't shards of ice. They were morning. "You've taken care of us," he said quietly.

"Happily," she responded with a smile. Her fleeting sense of grouchiness had passed since they first arrived. Their voices weren't the imaginary ones in her garden. Their hands could turn on the generator in the morning so she didn't wake up to darkness. Their smiles were genuine and warmed cold and feral places in her heart. "Bacon and eggs in the morning," she continued, excited to have an occasion that warranted those delicacies she'd been saving, "and then I'll show you what to do in the garden." There was always so much work—tilling, painting, repairing, pruning, cleaning. Having two more sets of hands would be lovely.

A quiet moan escaped Marcellus's lips at the mention of such a feast.

"What's your name?" Barnardo asked.

She flexed her jaw. This was the final test. Perhaps she would live alone again after all. Her answer of "three" earlier was premature.

"Ophelia IV," she answered honestly. It was a Resolute name.

"Hmm," Barnardo hummed, low, like a note on the cello. Then he looked up. "It's good to meet you, Ophelia."

She let out a relieved breath, taking his outstretched hand.

"Do we get to eat food from the garden?" Marcellus asked from behind him.

Ophelia laughed. "If you harvest it, of course. We'll start with tomatoes at breakfast."

"Fresh food," Marcellus exclaimed to Barnardo, as if he hadn't heard.

The older man's face melted into a relaxed grin. The lines on his cheeks weren't the mobile ones Marcellus had, but stricter ones used to famine and hardship.

"Tomatoes and bacon and eggs," she chanted. Maybe people liked meter too.

The next morning, at six forty-five, according to the clock, they sat to the promised meal. Marcellus helped her clear thirty-seven potion bottles and two field mice off the kitchen table. She really should have kept more of the potion-making supplies in the cauldron room, but the kitchen stove was such a cheery working area. She could look out the window and see Gertrude munching far too much lettuce, and Polonius trundling across the azaleas, and Daisy's spikes dashing across the stone path.

Eight hundred and sixty-seven days had been relatively the same. On the eight hundred and sixty-eighth day, Ophelia's life got even better. Still beautiful, still cozy, but no longer alone.

autumn surprise

music box

The red potion was gossiping again.

"And then," it whispered as Ophelia pushed cubed potatoes around the iron skillet, "a huge insect comes in here, it does. Some mutant or other. I'll wager it was those outsiders that brought it in."

"Oh, hush!" Ophelia snapped.

The whisps inside the bottle churned indignantly. "If you don't want to hear, don't ask," it said, huffy.

"I didn't ask." The cottage's kitchen was starting to smell pleasantly like char and onions.

"No one did," put in the metal-black potion.

"There was an insect, mark my words. Huge as a tower, with round eyes!"

Ophelia sighed, scooping potato chunks into three bowls. On went the onion sauce and a smattering of diced tomato and chive. "Don't be *an infinite and endless liar, an hourly promise breaker, the owner of no one good quality.*"

Her rhythmic warning made the black potion laugh,

but she thought she had maybe gone a bit too far. If Gertrude the rabbit had witnessed that observation, she would have been shocked.

"You know I don't mean it," Ophelia muttered on her way out. Truly, the day didn't make her grouchy at all, despite all this talk of enormous bugs invading her lovely cottage.

Today was the Autumn Equinox. No one could really be grumpy then.

She trundled through the burrow-like halls, balancing three hot bowls in her arms. "Breakfast!" she called.

Barnardo emerged from his bedroom, unburdening her of one helping of potatoes.

"Where's Marcellus?" Ophelia asked.

Barnardo's eyebrows rose, and he cast his white-blue eyes down the corridor. "Is he not with you? I told him to turn on the generator this morning—"

"Which was done."

"—and then see if you needed any help in the garden."

Ophelia frowned. "I haven't seen him."

The mystery was momentarily forgotten as Barnardo took a bite of the potato confection. She watched as his eyelids lowered and one corner of his lips turned up in a smile. He met her gaze and gave her a little nod.

But watching him reminded her that she could not tuck in to her own food because her hands were full. "I'm going to search for him. His potatoes are getting cold."

Without another word, she left, peering first into the cauldron room, then the sitting room, the curiosity corner, her own bedroom, scanning the garden, all to no effect. Few rooms remained. She turned the corner and—

"Eek!" She jumped back, nearly spilling the bowls of potato.

Marcellus raised his goggles. He sat in the middle of the round library. Books rose around him on shelves and at his feet lay a broken music box. Tiny springs haloed around the figurine of a ballerina. Absurdly big by comparison, Marcellus clutched a screwdriver in one hand.

"Sorry, Ophelia," he said.

She set down one of the bowls on the floor beside the broken music box. Relief and annoyed sadness made her give a harumph.

"I didn't mean to break it," he went on. Above the round goggles—which, for a moment, really did make him look like an insect—his hair stuck up at crazy angles. He waved the screwdriver through the air. "I've been trying to fix it. I promise."

"What's this?" cut in Barnardo's voice from behind her. It sounded suspiciously full of potato. He stopped short at the sight of Marcellus sitting on the floor.

"I thought I saw a frayed wire in the ceiling," Marcellus said penitently, lowering his eyes. "Then the ladder wobbled and I..."

"No harm done," said Ophelia, perhaps a shade too sharply. She loved that music box, and she knew Barnardo did too. "*You* don't have any broken bones, I assume?"

He shook his head ruefully.

Then a thought struck her. "Did you go messing about in the potion bottles? That's a dangerous business if you don't know what you're doing. The other day, a field mouse turned purple after scurrying over that table. Luckily, it had the sense to come back so I could set it right. The point is," she declared, refocusing on Marcellus, "you'd better let me handle any spellwork." She considered the mess of miniature pieces before her. A fixing spell might work to draw the items into their correct places...

"It's missing the gear that spins to match the music!" Marcellus burst out. He held together several of the pieces, as if Ophelia could see the ghostly outline of the parts that were missing. "I've never made one of these before, but it looks like the rotating drum that plays the music should encounter a gear attached to—"

"What size of gear?" Barnardo asked, his brows lowered.

Ophelia took her first heavenly bite of Autumn Equinox potato for breakfast, but she couldn't fully enjoy it with one of her lovely possessions—one that meant so much to Barnardo because of his lost daughter—broken into pieces.

Marcellus lowered his goggles over his eyes again and peered at the tiny machine. He made some measurements with an instrument he drew out of his pocket, first on his own littlest fingernail, then across up, down, and diagonal around the mechanism.

She found herself getting impatient. How precise could those measurements truly be? But Marcellus was a mechanic. He wasn't working up a spell, which could get finnicky with a wrong number attached.

Finally, he gazed up at them again, eyes magnified to bug-like proportions by the goggles. "Three millimeters."

Barnardo turned to Ophelia. The bowl in his hands was empty. Only the faintest glaze of onion sauce remained. "If you don't have one of those, I know where to find another."

Find another? Ophelia chewed thoughtfully. Almost nothing existed for miles, poisoned by the toxic air. Her cozy oasis was, for most purposes, all there was. "I don't think I have one."

Barnardo nodded solemnly, as if she had sent him on a quest.

"Do you know where to find another gear like that?" she asked.

"The airship," Marcellus answered for him.

Ophelia set down her spoon. This holiday was not going at all how she'd planned. Was Barnardo really thinking of leaving the bunker? "It's a shame about the music box," she said, "but it was an accident. I know Marcellus didn't mean to do it. We're all safe. No reason to put anyone in danger."

But Barnardo's expression only hardened with determination. She saw the military man, the ice-blue stare she'd noted when they first met. He had made up his mind.

"I'll go!" Marcellus declared, jumping to his feet and yanking off the goggles. He looked windswept and flushed.

"No." Barnardo gripped the edge of his bowl a little harder. "I'll take care of it. You fix it when I come back." With that, he gave Marcellus a meaningful stare.

Ophelia watched the two of them, trying to read their expressions. Barnardo's was both a command and a plea. Marcellus looked resigned.

"Ophelia, if you have any... extra way to keep me safe out there, I'll take it," said Barnardo, turning to her. "If not, I'm still going."

"Don't be absurd! It's the Autumn Equinox! I had lovely things planned for us all. If you get more toxin in your system, your bones might—"

"I know," he cut her off in a soft voice.

"Let him go, Ophelia," Marcellus said.

They were both so intent on this mission that she realized she could hardly stop them. "Then at least let me give you all the protection I can," she said, heart sinking.

CHAPTER 2

plans

Ophelia found the ancient scuba diving helmet she'd used herself while scavenging for parts. Its rusty hinges and smudged circular panel to see through didn't inspire confidence. It was warded by many spells, but they'd gone soft around the edges, and she didn't have time to tighten them all up.

Barnardo's determination to seek out that three-millimeter gear for the broken music box didn't waver, even after he saw what she presented as protection.

When she handed it over, it was hard not to picture the judgmental eyes of Polonius the badger, who trundled around a corner at that exact moment. "What poppycock!" he'd exclaim.

Daisy the hedgehog would shiver in her boots (if she had boots and had heard about Barnardo's bold decision.)

"Do not take this off," Ophelia directed, letting go of the unwieldy helmet. "How far is the airship?"

Barnardo glanced at Marcellus, who stood beside her,

then at his own fancy wristwatch. "I'll be back by six o' clock."

"Six!" Ophelia exclaimed. "But that's ages!" She calmed herself by taking a long breath of green-scented air.

"Be careful," Marcellus said, his mouth stretching into a long line that made him look even thinner, somehow.

Barnardo inclined his head, tucking the helmet under one arm. "Don't worry. I'll be safe."

"You'd better," Ophelia said, struck by a funny feeling in her throat and in the corners of her eyes. "Or else I'll turn your boots permanently wet. I'll name the patch of peppers after Marcellus instead of you."

Both men had taken pride in carving out that new section of the garden.

Barnardo's weathered face finally softened a little. Here was the friend Ophelia felt so privileged to have, the kind Barnardo, the one who wouldn't cause them any distress unless he felt it was important. "Six o' clock. I'll be here. Listen for the knock."

"Oh, I will," Ophelia said huffily, placing her hands on her hips. His kind reassurance just made her sorrier to see him go. And why was he so insistent about replacing a lost piece of her broken music box?

"Goodbye!" he said and turned to walk down the garden path. Past the thyme, wild roses, and fennel, past the pansies and primroses, past a frightened Daisy the hedgehog, past the tomatoes and onions, taking ninety-two steps, Barnardo walked to the edge of Ophelia's little world. He tugged open the door painted with trees and distant fairies, and disappeared.

Marcellus took Ophelia's hand. She squeezed it once before clearing her throat and rounding on him. "What is all this nonsense about retrieving that gear?" she asked, dusting off her palms just to give herself something to do.

The half-light of the string lights above the path and, higher, the blue glow worms, cast them both in a soft radiance. The garden was still lovely. Her cottage too. But the events of this morning felt like something had been pushed terribly off kilter.

"It's the Equinox, like you said," Marcellus answered. "Big day for him."

Ophelia puckered her mouth. "How?"

"It's his birthday."

"His birthday!" She plucked an elastic string from around her wrist and busily tied back her unruly brown hair. "Why did no one tell me?"

"I'm telling you now." Marcellus seemed much more confused than he should have been.

"What does that have to do with the gear?" she asked, deciding not to point out how dreadful it was that they hadn't told her the whole of their life story. Maybe that was a silly thing to get upset about. Barnardo's departure had left her raw.

"He thinks about the past on his birthday," Marcellus explained. "His family."

Ophelia had learned within a day or two of their arrival that the two men were not related, as she assumed. They had simply served in the same unit, and Barnardo had taken Marcellus under his wing. On missions, they became each other's family.

"Well, that simply won't do," she said briskly, beginning to feel like herself again. "It's a day for celebration—I already said it—and now we have more reason to celebrate than ever. Barnardo needs new memories."

"With new friends," Marcellus added.

Ophelia smiled, and a tuft of curly hair fell into her face. She blew it away. "Oh dear, we only have until six o' clock to make up a party for him."

"A party?" Marcellus laughed, but he looked not-so-secretly delighted by the idea.

Ophelia bustled inside with Marcellus at her heels. "Oh, a birthday party! There's so much to do. Too much... no, of course not. Barnardo deserves the best of parties and we will make it so."

She whirled, nearly bumping into the now-bewildered Marcellus. His pale, mobile face turned almost comical at her change in attitude.

"My my," she continued. Among all her private celebrations of the little joys in life, she had not hosted a birthday party in ages. "We must have cake, honey cake. Apple spritz. Oh, and pumpkin hand pies. Decorations, and... Marcellus! Why aren't you writing this down?"

His mouth opened and closed before he fumbled in his pockets. Finding nothing to write with, he cast her a guilty look.

Ophelia sighed, plucking a pad and pencil from a drawer by the sink. She thrust it into his hands and turned to re-light the stove.

"Candles." It didn't matter what the grumpy, safety-conscious Polonius might say. They simply must have them. "I have small ones in my bedroom side table."

She swept her gaze over the kitchen with its garden window, its herbs and cauldrons, utensils and mugs piled in the sink. The clutter of potion bottles watched expectantly. (Even the wispy red bottle had nothing to add.)

"Flowers. And hats!" She spoke as if to herself, but Marcellus scrawled furiously.

He held the pad awkwardly against his stomach, bending forward to write with one hand as if it would make him more helpful to have a hand free.

"My my. So much to do!" But her lips curled into a smile. Now the plans she'd made for the Autumn Equinox could be even bigger and better and more meaningful, because now they were to celebrate a friend.

She spent only ninety-eight more seconds filling out those plans, because time ran short and they had to get started.

Chest heaving as if he'd held his breath to complete the list, Marcellus palmed the pad of paper flat on the table. In spidery letters went the following list:

IN HONOR OF BARNARDO'S BIRTHDAY

- Honey cake with candles
- Apple spritz
- Pumpkin hand pies
- Flowers for table

- Party hats (three big & three small—extra smalls needed?)
- HAPPY BIRTHDAY sign
- Something with phonograph
- Deadline: 6:00

Ophelia didn't point out that the final item on the list was an important detail, not a task to complete. Despite the muddle of treasures she'd accumulated, she was essentially a lover of order, of everything being comfortably in its place.

"You have a phonograph?" Marcellus asked, a little out of breath.

"I don't often use it, but yes." She eyed the corner of the ceiling. Was that a cobweb?

"With records?"

"Of course with records," she snapped. "Barnardo will have music if he wants it. Or even if he doesn't."

A deep rumble issued from the stove. She shoved her hands in padded gloves and took a teapot off the heat. Grabbing two cups that went with the set (in that all three items had some kind of bird painted on them—did it matter that two depicted hummingbirds and the third a robin?) she poured herself and Marcellus a fortifying cup of cinnamon, clove, and Camellia tea.

Marcellus took his gratefully, and he groaned after taking a sip.

"And now," Ophelia said, eyes alight, "we get to work."

CHAPTER 3

treats

Marcellus waddled out of the back room in thick protective gear.

Ophelia stifled a smile as she met his eyes through the netting. "I didn't know you were afraid of bees."

"I'm not," he said. "I'm afraid of swarms of bees." His entire body was covered, but instead of a standard off-white beekeeper's outfit, he wore Ophelia's largest fluffy robe, high thick socks and boots, as well as a scarf and mittens. The only item that fit the image of a true beekeeper was the broad-brimmed hat with fine netting draped over it and elastic at the neck to keep it in place.

"Take care that honey doesn't get on those gloves," she chided.

"How much do we need?" He made his way to the counter where Barnardo's birthday party to-do list lay, as if it held the answer.

"One panel will be plenty." Standing before an orange pumpkin sitting near the list on the counter, she gripped the handle of a big knife in both hands, stabbed downward, and heaved her body weight forward to cleave it. Its outer rind split, creaking like a broken door. That wouldn't do. She couldn't keep practically jumping on the gourd to cut it to pieces. A sharpening spell was needed.

Marcellus made his way to the door leading to the garden. "Honey cake is his favorite," he murmured, as though steeling himself.

"See!" Ophelia cried, delighted. (She hadn't known Barnardo actually liked honey cake until then. She'd chosen it selfishly, because of its irresistible autumnal goodness.) "Now, enough dillydallying." And she shooed him out.

With Marcellus gone, she hustled to the crowd of potion bottles near the sink.

"Garlic," the ominous metal-black bottle said crossly.

She absently flipped the strand of garlic away from it. "Where is that amplifier?"

Most potions had a very specific purpose—curing the colds Polonius the badger sometimes contracted, disconnecting parts that had been glued together, creating a few square inches of fresh soil where none had been before—but the amplifier reacted to all simple spells and made them stronger. On her own, Ophelia could summon sparklers, almost like mini fireworks, but with the amplifier, that spell could make the sparklers grand enough to fill the Inner Box. In exchange for such generalized power, she had to keep the potion happy with offerings of dandelions and songs. If it didn't get a song a day, the charm would sputter. Fickle thing.

"A great while ago the world begun," she sang. *"With*

hey, ho, the wind and the rain." The clear, almost blue substance shimmered with delight. Ophelia kept her voice even, although privately she thought the potion was a little spoiled. *"But that's all one, our play is done, and we'll strive to please you every day."*

"You never sing us those songs," whispered the red bottle.

"Hush! Yes, I do." She scooped up the amplifier and poured out a drop on the knife's edge. Running a towel along it to spread the potion evenly, she noticed from the corner of her eye the timid Daisy sitting in the windowsill. The hedgehog's spines prickled. She was probably drawn by the song.

Ophelia set down the knife beside the pumpkin. "Come back at six and I'll have a treat for you," she said primly.

Daisy gave a small sniff of glee.

"Now, get on with you!" Ophelia ordered. "I have pumpkin to carve."

Then she sang another song to the amplifier while she prepared the pumpkin. She would need it for something much more difficult and impressive that evening. The other potions—the ones that were awake today—quietly groused about special treatment or hummed along.

A few minutes later, the pumpkin sizzled merrily in the oven, sprinkled with cinnamon, ginger, and nutmeg. Its delicious scent made Ophelia's mouth water as she bent over the triangles of tissue paper she'd cut with the point of the extra-sharp knife.

"Here!"

Ophelia looked up sharply as Marcellus entered, holding a big jar with chunks of honeycomb dripping with slow, golden goodness. She'd just finished writing the letter R in BIRTHDAY.

He set the honey on the counter, drew off the gloves (slightly sticky), and raised the netting around his face. His pale cheeks looked flushed. "There was a badger that kept growling at me while I got the honey," he explained.

"Polonius. He's protective of the hive."

"Well, it seemed like he wanted to punt me out of there so he could have it all to himself." He exhaled. "What are you cooking?"

"The pumpkin, of course. I'm about to start on the crust."

All his crabbiness disappeared, replaced with the beatific expression of someone expecting to eat a heavenly meal. Hopefully Barnardo would look just as delighted with their efforts.

Too bad he had to brave the poisonous outside world before he could enjoy it.

To distract herself from the thought, she cleared her throat and said, "Flowers, phonograph, apples. I suppose you know how to juice apples?"

Marcellus didn't answer.

She pointed to a makeshift juicer made of thick pieces of scavenged metal that she'd fashioned early in her residence at the cottage. "Use that."

Ophelia returned to making the banner, Marcellus replaced the fluffy robe with his own rabbit wool clothes and set out in search of flowers and apples, and desserts were soon baking in the oven. Curious birds appeared to watch the proceedings. Even Gertrude the rabbit stopped her munching—she was a menace to the garden, but Ophelia tried to turn a blind eye. Decorations were hung, music chosen, candles fetched. They agreed that Marcellus would answer the door when the inevitable knock came at six o' clock. He would lead Barnardo to the back entrance of the cottage so he could wash away the toxin in a specially prepared bath without revealing the birthday surprise too early. Then Barnardo would emerge, and voilà! The Autumn Equinox birthday party would commence.

Six o' clock arrived.

Barnardo did not.

At six o' five, Ophelia and Marcellus exchanged anxious looks. Had Ophelia simply assumed Barnardo would be punctual because he referred so often and so proudly to that wristwatch? She listened to the ticking seconds, to the hum of the generator, to the tinkle of magic in the honey-scented air.

Ophelia had not allowed herself to worry after determining to throw a party. Activity kept her breathless and frizzy and pleased throughout the day. Now, though, with no Barnardo, her heart darkened.

At six o' eight, the two of them stepped out of the cottage onto the garden path.

"He's fine. I'm sure," Marcellus said, glancing at her quickly, and then away toward the door to the outside. "He's tough as old boots."

Ophelia felt funny about being the one *comforted*

instead of *comforting*, but in that moment she was grateful too.

This time, Ophelia took Marcellus's hand for strength. As if sensing her unease, Daisy toddled close and shivered.

Where was Barnardo? All this for a tiny spring?

Finally, finally, at six nineteen, a knock sounded on the outer door.

CHAPTER 4

celebration

As much as Ophelia longed to answer the door with Marcellus to welcome Barnardo, she had to draw the bath. With Marcellus instructed to walk slowly back through the garden, she barely had time to get the water running and load the tub with Barnardo's favorite scrubs and towels.

She dashed to the kitchen, where she had the best view of the garden path. The two men approached the side of the house, Marcellus leading Barnardo to the back entrance. That way, he wouldn't see the birthday surprise they had in store. The older man looked like a spooky subterranean creature wearing that bubble of a scuba helmet.

Pivoting toward the counter, she rearranged the pumpkin hand pies, dusted with maple sugar. The letters in the sign needed separating. And—goodness alive!—the amplifier potion requested one more song. She sang it quickly and quietly as she cut a piece of the honey cake, crumbled it to pieces, and set it on the sill. The animals were all temperamental, liable not to come at all unless bribed.

One by one, they topped the sill, eager eyes alight. Gertrude the rabbit, who was the greediest eater, arrived first. Then came Daisy, who had known to expect some treat, and finally Polonius, looking exactly as if he'd been drawn out of his fireside armchair to investigate some disturbance only to find it was a present.

She popped the party hats on them, *one two three*, with not so much as a chirp of protest on account of the wonderful honey cake.

"He's here," Marcellus announced, entering the kitchen. He held a load of scraps and parts in his hands.

Ophelia pointed at them. "What's all that?"

"The ballerina," he answered, almost affronted.

Yes, of course! In all the excitement, Ophelia had nearly forgotten what kicked off the day's whirlwind. Barnardo had ventured out into the dangerous wastes for a tiny piece of the broken music box.

"Well, put it here," she said, clearing a space on the counter beside the vase of orange mums and yellow roses. Marcellus had told her a week or two ago that the object she used for a vase was actually a small cylinder liner. All she cared about now was that it looked festive. "Let's fix it before Barnardo comes out."

"He looked very pale."

"Yes, yes. So did you when you arrived here."

"He'll be all right, though." He set to work on the parts.

"Yes, he'll be all right."

Marcellus peered at the music box through the big,

round goggles, which he'd retrieved from where he left them in the library. Despite his difficulty that morning making any headway on the repair, now he seemed enchanted, filled with magic that encouraged pieces to fit and mend. Ophelia watched him, enraptured.

In no time at all, Marcellus straightened, wound the mechanism, and set the music box upright on the counter. Tinny music plinked out and, on top, a pink ballerina pirouetted, canopied by the bouquet.

Even Polonius paused his munching to look up when the music started.

Ophelia grinned at Marcellus. She hadn't wanted to admit how much she loved that music box before. Things got destroyed. One had to move on, make the most of life.

"It's wonderful," she admitted, touching it with the tip of a finger.

Barnardo's craggy face came into view at the kitchen entrance, flushed from the hot bath water. Ophelia and Marcellus straightened as if they'd been caught in a crime. The older man's mouth fell open as his gaze floated from the two of them, to the birthday sign, to the animals wearing their party gear, to the food, and, finally, to the music box.

"You fixed it," he said to Marcellus, but his throat sounded claggy.

"Happy birthday," Marcellus responded.

Ophelia jumped into action. "This is for you." She pushed a green party hat into Barnardo's hands. He almost dropped it in surprise. "And this." She poured apple spritzes for them all, *one two three*. The glassware didn't match.

Nothing matched here—not the plates waiting for their loads of pumpkin hand pies and honey cake, and not the three humans who formed this unlikely family.

"You put it on your head," Marcellus urged, holding back a laugh as he pointed at Barnardo's hat.

"You too," Ophelia ordered. She set down the spritz to fit her pointed purple hat in place. It bobbed atop the great fluff of her hair, which had long since wrestled free of its tie.

Finally, Barnardo's eyes seemed to clear and his voice came out stronger. "What is all this?"

"Why, your birthday, of course! It's the Autumn Equinox."

"I told her." Marcellus didn't look sheepish about this. He did, however, look pleasantly ridiculous in a pointed red hat.

Barnardo's lined face broke into a reluctant smile. "This took hard work."

"Worth it for a friend," said Ophelia.

"Cheers to that!" Marcellus cried, lifting his glass, obviously eager to try the spritz.

They clinked their glasses together and sipped the drink. It was all tiny popping bubbles and autumn sweetness. No one needed to tell them all to eat desserts next. Nothing would have stopped Marcellus, and, judging from the enormous slice of honey cake Barnardo took, nothing would have stopped him either.

The animals, still in the window in their party hats, hoping for more, watched their plates hungrily.

"Now," said Ophelia, turning to the badger, "I know you might not like this, sir, but it's a special occasion." At that, she produced a thin book of matches, struck a light, and lit the birthday candle. They'd forgotten to light it before eating, as eating was the more exciting activity. Ophelia and Marcellus wished Barnardo birthday blessings and he blew out the flame. The other two clapped.

"You didn't have to go through the trouble," Barnardo murmured around a bite of cake. His pale eyes looked deeper than usual, brows more mobile.

"Nonsense," Ophelia snapped. "I suspect you've gone too many birthdays without celebration. Another year among us is a treasure."

At the word *treasure*, Barnardo's eyes lighted on the music box again.

"I'm glad you knocked on my door," Ophelia went on, alarmed to find her eyes getting prickly for the second time that day. She knocked back the last of her second spritz. "I have one more surprise for you."

Marcellus knitted his forehead. "But there was nothing else on the list!"

"Nothing on *that* list," she said cryptically, as she left a few honey cake crumbs on the windowsill and marched toward the garden.

The men followed her, plates and glasses still in hand. She stopped at the threshold, looking out at the plants, the lights, the little extra flair she'd created here and there throughout the years. Gertrude the rabbit jumped from the sill, evidently realizing that they would get no more treats if they stayed there. (Ophelia had magicked the cottage in its earliest days not to allow in any creatures unless they were invited. Most of the creatures had found a way around this.

49

Daisy would almost certainly be snout-deep in a hand-pie by the time they made their way back inside.)

Ophelia sang, slyly drawing a small bottle from her sleeve.

"Now, my co-mates and brothers in exile,
Hath not old custom made this life more sweet?
The seasons' difference, as the icy fang
And churlish chiding of the winter's wind,
Which when it bites and blows upon my body
Even till I shrink with cold, I smile and say,
"This is our life, exempt from public haunt,
Finds tongues in trees, books in the running brooks,
Sermons in stones, and good in everything."

Marcellus and Barnardo stood as if entranced. With a flourish, Ophelia dabbed the amplifying potion on her fingers and flung it in an arc of droplets over the garden.

For a moment, nothing happened.

Then "ooh!" from Marcellus as autumn colors started at their feet and raced like fire through the entire garden. The leaves on the apple tree, on the ivy, on all the greenery turned flaming orange and cranberry red and lemon yellow.

Fortinbras the horny toad made a rare appearance from beneath a rock to cock his head slowly side to side, evaluating his new surroundings. Polonius snuffed.

Barnardo, wonderstruck as a child, watched until the finishing touches reached the tips of the leaves. "I didn't know you could do that," he breathed.

"It's the Autumn Equinox. It was going to be a surprise," Ophelia said, beaming.

"Shall we have a dance, then?" Marcellus suggested.

Ophelia had never seen him more excited, unless one counted the day of his rescue.

No one answered him, but he brought the phonograph outside anyway on its spindly little table.

As lively fiddle music played through the horn and the three of them linked arms, jumping and laughing in their absurd hats, dancing in the autumn leaves, Ophelia remembered the certainty she felt when she woke up this morning that today would be a good day.

She didn't know it would be better than that.

halloween spooks

CHAPTER 1

ghostly

Ophelia snuggled deeper into her armchair, feeling slightly naughty. Thick blankets couched her on all sides as she held a weighty black book of ghost stories. The original cover wore away before she found the volume, so in place of a title, she'd painstakingly outlined a silver ghost on the spine. Every time she read the book, the stories sent pleasant shivers up the back of her neck.

But none of that was why she felt like an impish child. It was two things, really. One—the candle. Try as she might to conserve them, the orange glow they cast, especially to illuminate spooky stories, made candles too cozy to pass up. Polonius the badger, who lived in her garden, would no doubt have been scandalized by her choice. Not to mention the occasional candles she used in the jack-o'-lanterns. Two —she was supposed to be cleaning and rearranging the potion bottles, not reading about Moaning Malcolm or the Senator's Ghost. All the potions got testy this time of year. After all, Halloween was only one day away.

She took a sip of elderberry tea and stubbornly continued reading. From her spot in the armchair, she could catch glimpses of dark hallways and odd shapes cast by the stuffed Elf Owl under its cloche or the fluttering pieces of sheet music she'd used to decorate an upper part of the wall near the library. With the main generator off for the night, shadows looked black as ink. A home for ghouls.

A footstep in the direction of the garden made her jump. *Enough of that*, she told herself. *It's only Marcellus or Barnardo.* But she couldn't focus on her stories anymore.

Closing the black-bound book carefully, she set it beside the tea. The silver ghost winked at her from its spine. She tucked the thick blanket underneath her chin and peered through the dusky opening to the kitchen. Why weren't the men appearing? For that matter, why were they awake at all? According to the clock with all the gears, it was eleven twenty-eight in the evening, only thirty-two minutes until Halloween.

"Ophelia." The voice belonged to Marcellus.

She exhaled. Silly to be spooked. "Yes?" she called back.

"Ophelia." Marcellus appeared at last, but his face looked even paler than usual and he held a stick with a net at one end. "I... thought I heard something," he said sheepishly.

She drew herself up. "Something big? Something small?" She gave the net a meaningful glare.

"I'm not sure," he admitted. "That's why I went to investigate."

Suddenly her heart seemed to grow too large for her chest. "Not outside?" she asked, though she could barely speak the words. The waste outside her little haven was dangerous, barren, and wild. If anyone knew she lived so comfortably in here...

"No. I don't think so."

"Good." She rose, taking the top blanket along with her. "Then what kind of noise are you talking about?"

"Like a..." His tall, thin frame shrank into itself. His off-white shirt (a repurposed uniform) hung oddly off his frame. "Like a faint scream."

"A faint scream?" Ophelia repeated, indignant. "Your mind is playing tricks. Maybe it was one of the animals?"

He held up the net like a wand. "It wasn't Gertrude or Daisy or Polonius." He named off the rabbit, hedgehog, and badger who lived in the garden.

"Then what do you think it was?" Ophelia asked. She did not like the notion of any ominous screams in her space.

He simply shrugged.

"It's just Halloween getting to you," she declared, forcing herself not to glance at the book of ghost stories again. She certainly wasn't scared of Halloween.

In quiet little shuffly noises, the potions in the kitchen complained. Their magic got wilder this time of year. October dimmed or magnified their power seemingly at random. She really ought to have soothed the crowd of little bottles instead of getting her mind all twisted up in phantoms.

"Let's go," she said suddenly, blowing out the candle.

Marcellus, used to responding to commands, obeyed immediately. The light in the cottage barely illuminated the rooms. There was the constant but faint blue glow from the faraway metal ceiling of the warehouse outside, and there were one or two lights she kept on inside the cottage so she was never in complete darkness. Otherwise, she'd bang her knee or something trying to get to the main generator in the morning.

The kitchen smelled softly of the apple cider she'd made earlier that day. Its crisp, warm scent bolstered her nerves.

"Are any of you making a ruckus?" she asked, glaring particularly at the metal-black potion that enjoyed the Halloween season the most. She knew because she kept catching it muttering little curses to itself, swirling and bubbling with too much glee.

No one answered. Marcellus eyed her sideways.

Outside the kitchen window, the outline of the garden was barely visible. Specters and ghosts from her story kept crowding into her mind like bees to a hive. It didn't help that she'd created a garland of pumpkins and skulls to festoon the space above the stove. Raggedy black fabric, artistically torn, acted like a huge spider web in the opposite corner. Next to a plate of pumpkin bars and a dish of pumpkin bread pudding (probably growing slightly stale, despite the caramel sauce) sat a pointed witch's hat. Ophelia didn't wear such things, but she owned one partly for a laugh and partly for Halloween decoration.

She'd magicked more pumpkins than usual to grow in the garden since she had company this Halloween, so jack-o'-lanterns sat by twos and threes all over the house. She had been so excited by the idea of more pumpkins that she'd accidentally let the vines get out of control. Marcellus had helped her construct tall structures for them to climb so they didn't take over the garden. Daisy the hedgehog, who used to like pumpkins, now trembled a little when she saw yet another orange gourd growing high in the air, as if it already had an evil carved grin.

Ophelia shook her head. Wavy brown curls fluffed around the blanket she still held around herself like armor. Turning back to Marcellus, she said, "The cottage makes strange noises sometimes, just like I'm sure your airship did."

He nodded but pursed his thin lips.

"There can't have been a scream," she said.

"Who's screaming?" asked a low, raspy voice. Barnardo, the owner of the voice, appeared in the kitchen doorway, his back military-straight. His concerned expression and hastily tugged-on robe showed he was tired, though. It was late.

"No one," said Ophelia.

"I heard something." Marcellus shot Ophelia an apologetic look. "I really did. I'm just not sure what it was."

"Then we'll find out," Barnardo declared. Only the faintest slump of his shoulders suggested how reluctant he was to search outside instead of going back to sleep.

Marcellus brightened, fingers tensing on the handle of the net. "It won't take long. Maybe Ophelia's right."

Ophelia frowned. It wouldn't have hurt him to admit that when it was only the two of them talking.

Barnardo raised his eyebrows at her.

"I suppose I should come too," she said, considering whether to bring the blanket wrapped around herself.

"Sooner to get this mystery solved," Barnardo urged.

She sighed. "Fine." With a glance at the quiet potions, she added, "That scream had better not be real."

A potion bottle in the back let out a puff of sparkly black smoke. Then everything—the cottage, the garden, and the three sleepy people standing in the kitchen—were plunged into absolute darkness.

CHAPTER 2

dark

Under the windowsill, Daisy the nervous hedgehog squeaked in alarm. Why she was so scared, Ophelia didn't know. Hedgehogs were used to the dark, weren't they? The three people in the cottage were the ones who should be really frightened.

Ophelia gripped the blanket more tightly around her shoulders. In the one thousand and eleven days since she'd finished the cottage, the lights had never gone out. Wires in the ancient warehouse ceiling emitted enough low-level power to keep a light or two on all the time. What had happened?

A shuffling noise to her right, followed by a series of grunts and a curse worthy of the metal-black potion bottle, culminated in the question, "Where are the matches?"

Luckily, she'd kept them in her capacious pocket the whole time. Shock had frozen her so thoroughly that she hadn't had the presence of mind to fish them out right away.

"Here," she answered, drawing one out. Rather than reaching for Barnardo's hand to give him the match, she whispered to it, "*O for a Muse of fire, that would ascend the brightest heaven of invention.*" Spells liked poetry.

Usually.

The darkness remained stubbornly in place.

"What are you doing, Ophelia?" Marcellus asked.

"I'm lighting a match."

"Can't you light it against the table?" Barnardo said.

She'd never tried doing it that way. But instead of trying Barnardo's method, her stubbornness reared up, fueled by the fright she'd received when the lights went out. She could perform a simple lighting spell. All it took was a dash of the sunlight magic she used to keep the garden alive. Simplicity itself.

"*So many journeys may the sun and moon make us again count o'er ere love be done!*"

After a tense moment during which they stood in breathless silence in darkness so black they couldn't so much as make out each other's outlines, Marcellus asked, "Is something supposed to be happening?"

"Of course something is supposed to happen!" Ophelia snapped back. Why wasn't the spell working? Was Halloween playing havoc with her magic?

Finally, her eyes began to adjust enough to trace the window to the garden. The blue glow worms high above turned the plants faintly gray.

The trellised pumpkin vines outside looked like the faint outline of monsters.

"Give me the match, Ophelia." Barnardo said it kindly,

but her mood darkened all the same. Her way of conjuring a flame should have worked. It always had before. And the lights had always worked too.

Grumpy with fright and a new powerlessness, she handed over the match. Judging from the scraping noises, it wasn't easy for Barnardo to light the flame either. Ophelia shouldn't have felt glad, but the night had made her petty.

Finally, a little orange flame burst into light. Ophelia brought three of her precious candles and Barnardo lit one for each of them. Happily, she kept all her candles in little stands so no one had to hold onto the wax and get finger burns.

Grimly, she dragged the blanket back and slung it across the armchair. She had a feeling they'd still go on a search for the mystery noise.

The two men stood in silence, waiting for her return. On the edges of candlelight, vague shapes of cobwebs, pumpkins, and potion bottles blossomed.

The wispy red potion murmured something about the lights being the blue potion's fault. It only got halfway through its complaint when Ophelia spoke up. "Well, let's go then." If anything, they needed to turn on the main generator to get the other one up and running.

Marcellus swallowed.

At the last second, Ophelia grabbed a pumpkin bar and stuffed half of it into her mouth for courage. The others acted as if they'd been ordered to do the same, because Marcellus set down his net and Barnardo took two with one hand. Armed with candles and mouthfuls of pumpkin dessert, the three of them set out into the garden.

On normal nights, Ophelia admired the blue glow high above, but it had been a long time since she'd really noticed how much like a galaxy it looked. Above the darkened flowers, above the tall structure lumpy with pumpkins, the only visible color was that unearthly blue. The others looked up too, underlit by candle flame.

Daisy scuttled out from under the window and knocked gently against Ophelia's slipper. Ophelia crammed the rest of the pumpkin bar into her mouth and scooped up the hedgehog, settling her on her shoulder. Spines softly poked Ophelia's cheek when she turned her head, but Daisy, trembling, tried very hard to be still.

"It's okay," Ophelia murmured to the hedgehog, who had never shown this level of fright before.

They headed first to the big generator. It was unsightly, so Ophelia had built up the cottage and garden around it to hide its big, blocky form. A lever stuck out from the side. With a familiar groan, the lever protested as Ophelia yanked it down.

Nothing.

This concerned her more than the lights in the house going out. What was going on?

"So, this scream," prompted Barnardo in a normal voice that sounded loud because of how dark it was. "Could you tell where it was coming from?"

Marcellus seemed much more at ease now that they were outside looking for the source of the sound. Maybe he had acted like this on the airship too—nervous until the moment came to take action. "Out here," he said. "I couldn't tell exactly where it came from. I only stuck my head out the window to look and then went to tell Ophelia."

"Did you see anything out the window?" Ophelia asked.

He shook his head. "Everything looked normal."

Together, they walked slowly and carefully through the garden, casting the candlelight into far corners of the path.

Polonius the badger, Ophelia thought, was probably sitting before the fire in his den at that moment. He had the right idea. Picturing him wearing miniscule eyeglasses so *he* could read ghost stories made her smile. Of course, he'd never read anything so fanciful as ghost stories. Mysteries, perhaps.

They passed beds of thyme, the mushroom sculpture with snails on it, and strings of bulbs with no life in them.

They muttered things like "anything over there?" and "is that something?" and "it's hard to see."

"Maybe if we're quiet," Barnardo suggested, "the noise will happen again."

Privately, Ophelia wondered if this hubbub was for nothing after all. They hadn't heard strange sounds. The only weird thing about the night was the power going out and her inability to fix it. Maybe if she used some of the amplifier potion and tried again...

"Sounds good," Marcellus agreed.

"Fine," said Ophelia.

They stopped walking and listened.

CHAPTER 3

bubble and trouble

I n the silence, Ophelia watched the flicker of the candlelight play across the faces of Marcellus and Barnardo. She thought about the ghosts in her stories. She wondered if it was officially Halloween yet, and if it was, how she would celebrate in the morning.

If there was morning.

Time was a funny thing when one lived in a cottage inside a warehouse inside a bunker. No natural light came in. Ophelia herself provided the sunlight energy needed to grow the plants, and two generators worked to power the lights, electricity, and hot water. Now, her magic had gone wonky (she tried thinking a small spark into her hand but nothing happened) and both generators had gone out.

Would Halloween be totally dark, with only candles providing light to see the jack-o'-lanterns and cups of apple cider? It was like the tales of what life was like before conflict in Denmark brought on all this chaos.

Ophelia shivered, and it wasn't a pleasant shiver this time. On her shoulder, Daisy shivered too.

"Oh my!" Ophelia could practically hear Daisy squeak. "Isn't this just dreadful? Just dreadful!"

She raised a hand and gently ran a finger over Daisy's spikes to calm her.

Only the sound of Gertrude the rabbit rustling through the vegetables broke the silence that normally hummed with the generator and her sparkly magic.

Then...

"Eek! Eek!"

All of them (including Daisy) snapped their heads up toward the sound. A slight pulse like the generator beat the air.

Barnardo raised his candle. A dark shape whooshed over the pumpkin structure.

"That's it!" Marcellus cried.

A second shape glided after the first.

"Eek! Eek!"

The cry did sound a little like a scream, but Ophelia had heard that sound before. It wasn't human.

It was a bat.

The bats whirled around, making a big circuit above the cottage then over the mass of pumpkins.

"They're bats!" she said in wonder. How had they managed to get in?

"Bats?" Marcellus asked.

The way he asked it made it sound as if he'd never heard of the creatures before. Education had really gone to seed.

"You know," she said, "like mice with wings?"

"I know what bats are," he replied. "I've just never seen one."

"We haven't gotten a good look yet," said Barnardo pragmatically. His light blue eyes looked spooky in the darkness, almost glowing.

They all raised their candles a little higher.

"Eek! Eek!"

Ophelia couldn't help feeling very satisfied with this conclusion. Halloween was... today, probably, and bats were flying around her cottage? How marvelous! This revelation didn't solve the problem of the broken generators or haywire magic, but it was certainly better than any other alternative explanations for screams.

The two bats swooped down over their heads. As one, Ophelia, Marcellus, and Barnardo ducked. Daisy clung to Ophelia's shoulder for dear life.

"I shouldn't have left the net," said Marcellus.

"Nonsense!" Ophelia snapped, straightening again. "No one is capturing these bats. If they have found a way inside, then they are part of the family."

"The problem is," Barnardo said, "they are probably the ones who messed up the wires."

Ophelia considered this. Finally, she said, "I agree. That is unacceptable. I'll have to teach them where they are not supposed to go. Bat guano is natural fertilizer, you know."

She'd owned a rack of bat wings since before she began building the cottage. The person who sold it to her rambled on about how guano improved soil but burned through a number of other things. Ophelia couldn't remember all the items the woman had mentioned, but wiring certainly wouldn't have been surprising.

She sighed. "Well, shall we get inside?"

The men didn't take much convincing, especially since there was pumpkin bread pudding in there, and deep blankets, and pillows, and hot cider, and even ghost stories if they wanted any more. She doubted she could sleep. Instead, she needed to get to the bottom of her magic running out. The generators could be fixed. (The hazy outline of a plan was forming in her mind. It involved Marcellus and a long, sturdy ladder.)

"Bats!" Barnardo exclaimed as they stepped back inside the warm kitchen.

Ophelia offered to pluck the hedgehog off her shoulder at the threshold, but Daisy refused to budge. "Bats don't eat hedgehogs," Ophelia explained, but she got only a sniff in reply.

"How do you think they got in?" Marcellus asked.

"Maybe there's a weak point in the ceiling," Ophelia guessed.

"We'll get that patched up for you," said Barnardo. His confidence warmed her insides.

Marcellus smiled. "Yeah. I used to do all kinds of crazy repairs in the air."

Barnardo nodded gravely. It was obvious he took pride in his young comrade's work.

"Perfect!" said Ophelia, bustling to the cider bottle and pouring herself a glass. "I'll make sure the plants survive." That sounded better somehow than *I'll fix my broken magic.* "And our new bat friends."

"Bat friends?" Marcellus said doubtfully.

"I'm thinking Bubble and Trouble."

Barnardo let out a rich laugh. "Do you give everything a name?"

"Most things with life and a personality," she replied.

By the time they all had a satisfying cup of cider, they were yawning and thinking of bed. Repairs could wait till morning.

"How late is it?" Ophelia said creakily through a massive yawn.

Barnardo consulted his watch. "One thirty-two."

"Good heavens!" she exclaimed. "Get to bed, both of you. Shoo!" One candle remained lit, placed in the center of the table. Pumpkins grinned at them from shadowy corners. "And happy Halloween!"

CHAPTER 4

halloween

Ophelia's eyes shot open. Light blazed through her cozy room, gilding the blankets, falling on framed pictures of moonlit forests wreathed in mist and clusters of mushrooms and dancing couples and maps of improbable places like Poland. Light fell on a small, double-sided, oval-shaped picture by her bedside of lost faces of family. It fell on the small hedgehog curled up beside the frame. It fell on a clutch of three pumpkins in the corner and a rush of bats she'd attached to the wall.

Bats. Lights.

She flipped off the covers and shoved her feet into fuzzy slippers. "Marcellus?" she called as she exited the room.

The generator must have been fixed. Last night, everything had been so dark. She almost missed that nighttime darkness, but having power was much more important.

She didn't see Marcellus or Barnardo by the armchair or their room or the kitchen (though half the bread pudding was gone.)

"First things first," she muttered, setting a fragrant log in the kitchen fire and warming a kettle. In minutes, she completed her morning ritual by filling a mug with her favorite autumn tea. The steam tickled her nose and warmed her cheeks.

Armed with the hot mug, she ventured outside. Strings of bulbs buzzed as they illuminated the garden path. The pumpkin trellis looked friendlier than it had against the blackness last night. These pumpkins wouldn't stick out scarecrow arms or top the Headless Horseman's neck. They'd be smiling jack-o'-lanterns or pies.

"Marcellus?" she called again.

"Over here," came the rich, raspy voice of Barnardo.

She made her way to the generator they turned on every morning to find Barnardo standing like a soldier in front of it and Marcellus climbing down from on top, smudged with grease and wearing a huge grin.

"Fixed it!" he announced.

"That's brilliant," Ophelia declared.

Marcellus jumped down. He clutched a wrench in one hand. "No problem. I just had to check the ignition coil and the air filter. There was carbon buildup in a couple places. Oh, and I found something to replace the flywheel. That generator has seen better days." As he listed problems with the machine, he looked nothing but pleased. Ophelia suspected that he'd be happy to fix the generator every week, if it ever came to that.

"So it should work perfectly now," Barnardo concluded before Marcellus could launch into more detail.

Now that her eyes had adjusted, everything didn't seem

so bright. The garden had the dawn-and-dusk glow she loved. Mist lay at the far end. Snuffling through the leaves near the beehive, Polonius trundled with purpose as if he too had been woken up by the lights.

Ophelia sipped her tea. "Good timing," she said. "I'll have you build a bat house next, so Bubble and Trouble don't have to live in the ceiling."

Marcellus nodded. She got the feeling that, although he liked the idea of building, he didn't like the idea of bats. When he wiped his forehead, more grease smeared across it.

"Clean up," she said. "It's Halloween." She didn't elaborate but, as usual, she'd planned surprises.

Together, they made their way inside the cottage. Marcellus ate another helping of bread pudding before leaving to wash. Barnardo disappeared for a while too. Ophelia sent him with tea.

When Ophelia was alone once more in the kitchen, the potion bottles on the counter all began exclaiming and murmuring and singing softly at once, as she'd anticipated.

"You've been naughty," she told them, cross that she couldn't use her magic yesterday when she'd badly needed it.

"It's the blue potion's fault," accused the wispy red potion. "They started it, they did." That was impossible. The blue potion wasn't sentient like many of the others. Besides, all the bright blue potion could do was untie knots.

"Oh hush," said Ophelia.

"*Fair is foul, and foul is fair; hover through the fog and filthy air,*" chanted the metal-black potion unhelpfully.

Ophelia reached for a bottle that looked like liquid gold.

"You never choose me," said the wispy red potion.

"Or me!" added a square bottle with a gloppy green substance inside. Had she ever heard that one speak?

"That's because you are for emergencies," Ophelia explained. "Defense, pest control, that kind of thing."

"But it's Halloween," said a few.

All magic wanted to be used on Halloween. What made that tricky was that magic tended to be in a mischievous mood, especially that night. Portraits blinked, shadows danced, and phantom voices sang.

Ophelia started to sense that sparkle in the air that had been missing last night. She had to be careful not to let any spells get out of control, but hopefully her own magic had returned. Before last night, it had never gone completely, and the sensation left her feeling vulnerable.

On a whim, she set down her tea, swept up the witch's hat, and settled it on her head. Taking the cork off the golden potion, she murmured softly to it while swishing it clockwise eight times, "*Light thickens, and the crow makes wing to th' rocky wood.*"

One by one, pumpkin faces glowed from within. She watched them bloom across the kitchen, into the hall, and out in the garden.

Her magic was back.

The book she read last night had given her an idea. Swiftly, she ran to her cauldron room, taking stock of all the ingredients on the shelves. She didn't go in there nearly enough, she decided. Not only was it cozy as a woodland apothecary, but it was appropriately creepy for Halloween as well. Also, the levels of chamomile and dried lizard scales had become unconscionably low. She would deal with that later, when Marcellus was working on the roof's wiring in a few days.

She chose the smallest cauldron—not the large one in the center of the room. On a day like today, a spell that big was likely to explode and turn them all green or something.

A few minutes later, the cauldron boiled with a pinch of this, a pinch of that. None of the potions in the kitchen could produce the illusion she wanted for tonight. Before Barnardo and Marcellus arrived, there was little need for such theatrics (although she sometimes created fun illusions for herself to pass the time.)

"*Thrice to thine and thrice to mine and thrice again to make up nine,*" she sang, stirring the brew. The steam began to take shape. It grew thicker and whiter. She turned off the light. Up from the cauldron rose the wavering, floating shape of a smiling ghost, illuminated from within.

She smiled and winked at it. The ghost winked back. "Perfect!" she said. "Now—"

"Eek!" came a squeak from the other room, louder than it had been last night.

Ophelia turned the light on again and headed back to the kitchen. The friendly ghost illusion followed behind her.

She entered the cider-smelling kitchen just in time to see the two bats settle upside-down into the top corner, wrapping their gray, membranous wings around themselves.

"Bubble!" she scolded. "Trouble! You're not allowed inside the house."

They shifted their weight on little clinging feet.

Ophelia exhaled. "All right. But only today! Right now, you can fetch Marcellus and Barnardo for me."

They promptly flew down the hallway, wings flapping. The ghost watched them go.

"And you," Ophelia said to it, "join us for today."

The metal-black potion bottle made a barely audible sound of approval.

From down the hall, Marcellus yelped. He soon appeared, fleeing from his bat pursuer. Barnardo entered after him. His steps tripped along faster than Ophelia had ever seen him move. The bats landed in the corner again, eyeing them all.

"Come on," said Ophelia, turning off the lights and letting the pumpkins glow brighter.

"Is that...?" Marcellus stared at the ghost floating beside her. He looked white as chalk.

"An illusion," she explained. "No one dead. He's friendly."

The ghost gave a little bow, or at least seemed to waver at the waist.

"I forget you're a witch," said Barnardo.

She cocked a brow at him. "With all these potions around? And what fun is it if I can't be extra witchy on Halloween?" She remembered the pointed hat she wore and laughed.

Marcellus and Barnardo chuckled too, though

Marcellus sounded a little unsure of all this ghost and bat business.

To calm his nerves, she opened up a cabinet door to reveal the secret treats she'd made the day before. There were apple tarts that looked like tombstones, ghost-shaped cookies, popcorn with a drizzle of caramel, onion and sage pinwheels, and, of course, pumpkin pie, complete with a skull design made of sugar.

"Ophelia!" Marcellus breathed, helping her bring out each plate and set it on the table. "It's wonderful."

"Magical," she agreed, quite pleased with herself.

Even the ghost, translucent in the jack-o'-lantern light, acted impressed.

They each took an apple tart. Barnardo's was halfway to his mouth when Marcellus held his aloft. "To Ophelia and a happy Halloween!"

She lifted hers up to tap against the crust of the others and added, "And to Marcellus, who fixed the generator and introduced us to two new friends!"

For a moment, he looked confused. But then Barnardo rolled his eyes, smiling faintly, and said, "To us all... even Bubble and Trouble."

Ophelia grinned as the bats flapped once in acknowledgment, and the ghost wobbled happily in the air, and they all took big bites of the magnificent apple tart.

Outside, in the dark, the pumpkin structure looked moonlit in the blue glow.

lost hedgehog

ingredients

Ophelia bent over her cauldron, trying to recall ingredients.

"Wolfsbane, toe of frog, eye of bat..."

She stirred absently and pushed a curl of hair out of her eye. After making this potion so many times, the recipe should have been firmly lodged in her memory. In retrospect, it was silly not to have written down recipes for all the potions she regularly used. She just assumed she would remember.

She bit her lip, her eyes roaming over the miniature shelves filled with ingredients. Too many of the bottles were empty. Nine out of forty-one, to be precise. What kind of witch was she when she didn't keep her witchiest room stocked?

There and then, she decided that she needed to raid her garden for the ingredients she needed. Too bad that she'd been making this potion for her garden in the first place. Her plants needed more space, especially now with

Barnardo and Marcellus eating and using up energy. Her garden wasn't big enough anymore.

She looked down at the faintly bubbling silver liquid. It reminded her of the ghost apparition she'd conjured for Halloween. That shivery, floating ghost was such a festive addition to the day.

But you won't be able to re-create it without more ingredients.

That settled it. She gave the brew four more clockwork strokes, whispered a four-line poem to it with four metrical feet in each line (spells loved numbers and meter), and hung up the big spoon on a hook. That should be enough to ensure the potion didn't go rancid while she hunted for the remaining ingredients.

Bustling out of the little cauldron room, she instantly smelled mint and bramble tea. The smell was followed by the sight of a tall man rounding the corner, cupping a mug in one hand.

"Barnardo!" she greeted.

He smiled. "Ophelia. Everything all right?"

"Would you like to help me collect ingredients today?"

His mouth turned down, considering. "I don't see why not."

"What's going on?" Marcellus poked his head into the hallway. He'd been in the library, one of his favorite rooms, probably tinkering.

"I need ingredients from the garden," she said.

Marcellus dusted off his hands and approached. "I'll get them for you."

"We can all get them. It'll go faster that way." Ophelia

secretly thought it would be more enjoyable to gather them all together too.

Barnardo checked his fancy wristwatch as if he planned to time them covertly.

"What do you need?" Marcellus asked.

"Eye of bat—"

Barnardo frowned. "What?"

"Bubble and Trouble?" Marcellus chimed in. "You need their *eyes*?"

Ophelia hadn't felt the stigma of being a witch since she first invited the men to join her in the little cottage paradise she'd created. But the way they both pinned her with aghast stares made her huff.

"Of course that's not what I mean!" Bubble and Trouble—the bats who had found their way into the bunker on Halloween—were her friends, just as Daisy the hedgehog or any of the other garden animals were. She didn't see much of the two bats, but Marcellus had constructed a little house for them on the apple tree at her instruction. Sometimes they heard them squeak and shriek outside as they flapped around. "Eye of bat is a plant. *Cuphea Ilavea*."

Marcellus raised an eyebrow, clearly skeptical.

Perhaps she should start keeping the nicknames of the plants to herself. "I'm not going to hurt any of the animals," she said, rolling her eyes. They couldn't think she'd actually do that. "I need dried herbs and spices, for the most part."

Barnardo sipped his tea, his eyes twinkling. "That won't be a problem."

"Some of them are near Daisy's burrow or the beehive."

"I don't have to wear that suit again, do I?" asked Marcellus, who had collected honey before to Ophelia's great amusement.

Ophelia allowed a pause before she assured him that he didn't need to collect honey or the plants around the hive if he didn't want to. She or Barnardo could handle that part.

She clapped her hands together. "I'm working on a potion that will make the garden bigger—more space for all of us—so I say we get going."

Marcellus's expression snapped back into eagerness.

"I'll get the ingredients around Daisy's burrow," Ophelia went on. She hadn't seen the hedgehog for a few days and needed to check on her anyway. It wasn't like Daisy to be away for so long. Even though she acted skittish, she always wanted to be involved in what Ophelia and the others were doing. "Barnardo, do you mind gathering ingredients around the hive?"

He finished his tea in one gulp. "Not at all."

"Good. Marcellus, you'll get the rest. Let me write them down for you." She moved past them into the kitchen where she kept some loose sheafs of paper.

BARNARDO'S LIST

1. Sage leaves
2. Pollen
3. Five aster blooms

MARCELLUS'S LIST

1. *Cuphea Ilavea* (NOT real bat eyes—look at the plant and take the part that LOOKS like eye of bat)
2. Snakeroot (do NOT eat)
3. Bulbous buttercup flowers and leaves (the stem looks like a frog's foot)

OPHELIA'S LIST

1. 34 poppy seeds
2. Wolfsbane
3. Scale of dragon / tarragon
4. Check on Daisy

Ophelia gave them each the bottles and materials they would need, and together they traipsed out into the garden.

Marcellus showed his list to Barnardo, then turned to Ophelia. "Why would I want to eat snakeroot?"

"Many of the flowers on these lists are edible," she explained, "just *not* that one."

Ophelia ignored the mutterings of the wispy red potion who claimed in a whispery voice that the new potions would take the place of old ones that would get thrown out. The attention-loving amplifier seemed very concerned about this possibility.

Then Ophelia spied a field mouse picking its way among the chaos of bottles on the counter, and that was enough to turn the outraged attention of the potions elsewhere.

Armed with a tiny stoppered bottle and a basket, Ophelia broke off from the others down the garden path. She could imagine Daisy protesting that anyone should bother checking on her—she was perfectly all right. But, despite the garden's lovely green smell and the blooms and vegetables and glowing lights, Ophelia felt a twist in the pit of her stomach. How long had it been since she'd seen her favorite hedgehog? A week?

She picked up her pace.

"Daisy!" she called under her breath.

Finally, the entrance to the burrow came into view. Or at least where the burrow used to be. Now there was only a disturbed pile of earth there, as if a giant foot had smashed it down.

CHAPTER 2

missing

Ophelia covered her mouth, distress growing like a balloon inside her. She crouched beside the disturbed earth that had once been the entrance to Daisy's hedgehog burrow. With one hand, she rooted around, but it was no use. The fresh dirt hadn't just covered the entrance. There was no more hole there. So where was Daisy?

A spell rose to mind, and Ophelia sang softly to the earth of the garden.

"Without the bed her other fair hand was,
On the green coverlet, whose perfect white
Showed like an April daisy on the grass..."

Leaves rose into the air and swirled. Ophelia held her breath. She could easily imagine Polonius the badger leaning back in an armchair before a hearth fire, saying, "Perfectly good burrow. That's what you get for meddling."

But who had meddled? Ophelia couldn't conceive of Barnardo or Marcellus doing this to Daisy on purpose. So far, she'd only seen Daisy's home destroyed. Hopefully that didn't mean that the timid creature was gone too...

Ophelia cleared her throat and stood, scanning the ground. Gertrude the rabbit stuck her head above the greenery with wide-eyed curiosity, but there was no sign of Daisy.

Ophelia glanced at her list, mentally checking off the last item that read *Check on Daisy*. That task hadn't gone well. Concern for Daisy overshadowed everything else. Who cared about poppy seeds when her friend might be in danger?

"Can you see Daisy?" she called over the garden to the others.

Barnardo popped up with a fistful of sage. "No. Is everything all right?"

After him came Marcellus, farther away. "Is this the part that's supposed to look like eyes?" he asked, pointing down to a plant she couldn't see.

"Pause that. We need to find Daisy."

Marcellus wiped one hand off on his pant leg. "The hedgehog?"

"Of course," she snapped. "She's missing."

Marcellus's voice sounded thin so far away. "Do you have a way of finding her?"

A way of finding her.

Ophelia snapped her fingers. "Yes! Let me get a spell together." She ran through the bottles of potions sitting on the shelf. Would any of them work to locate Daisy? She knew location spells, but most of them were for finding objects—lost coins, a favorite skirt, a flower planted in the wrong place—not for finding lost animals. Most potions and spells were very specific, even finnicky about things like the distinction between plants and animals. She bit her lip. "Hurry up with the ingredients," she called.

Polonius the badger lumbered, snuffling, into view.

"Do you know where Daisy is?" she whispered.

His only reply was to turn his stripey head in her direction briefly before shuffling on.

"You're no help."

She hadn't realized until now how much she counted on Daisy to be there. Her nervous little squeak at sudden noises, her tiny bead of a nose sniffing flowers, her spiny back trundling through beds of veggies... No more hedgehogs existed that Ophelia knew about to replace her if she was—

"Poppycock!" she said aloud, cutting off that train of thought. As if Daisy could be replaced. All the hedgehogs in the world couldn't do that. They'd be undeniably cute, but there was no one like her Daisy.

In record time (eight minutes and twelve seconds, give or take) Ophelia gathered the three ingredients on her list. She counted out poppy seeds on her palm. They rolled about maddeningly, obscuring their number, so she had to drop them one by one, just so she could be sure she'd gathered thirty-four. Then she funneled the seeds into a skinny bottle. Wolfsbane and tarragon came next.

A glance showed that Marcellus had finished his tasks too, even if his expressive face demonstrated far too much uncertainty about whether he'd done it correctly. Barnardo daubed a tiny bottle against the center of a few flowers for the pollen. Not the best method, but he could still gather the pollen she needed that way.

Good. Everyone was nearly finished.

She brought her ingredients back inside, through the kitchen door, down the hallway to the cauldron room. Some of the louder potions called faintly after her as she passed.

"Not now," she murmured, her thoughts too full of her nervous, spiky friend.

Each ingredient belonged in a particular slot on the little shelves lining the walls. Hurriedly, she placed a bottle there, a flower there. She was happy to see that the potion she'd been working on hadn't gone bad in her absence, but did she really need that now? The garden could grow larger any day.

Ophelia rolled up her sleeves and attempted to tuck her curly hair behind her ears. Her library held a grimoire or two. She might need those since she'd never tried concocting a location spell for a living being.

Or I could try scrying. The trouble with that plan lay in the preparations she'd need to make. They took too long. At least, the impatience swirling inside her didn't like the idea.

She drummed her fingers against the lip of the large cauldron. "I hope you aren't in danger," she muttered. "Foolish hedgehog..." It was a term of frustrated endearment, and a hard lump settled in the center of her throat.

She's fine. She must be.

Settling on a spell that was a combination of others

she'd tried before, she started adjusting the mixture in the cauldron.

She was seven stirs into the first phase of the potion when Barnardo and Marcellus appeared with their spoils. A corner of the list Ophelia had given him stuck out of Marcellus's pocket. "Here you go, Ophelia," he said quickly, offering what he had.

"Sage, pollen, aster, snake, bat, frog," she recited, pointing to each blank space on the shelves in turn.

Marcellus looked dubiously at the ingredients in his hand as if they would suddenly transform from plants to something venomous that might strike.

"I hope you find Daisy," Barnardo said, placing the aster blooms in their place. A crease formed between his eyebrows. The men hadn't spent as much time with her garden friends as she had, but they still knew them all by name.

Ophelia nodded, adding some dried dandelion greens to the swirling brew. "So do I."

CHAPTER 3

Search

Ophelia was making this up as she went along. Too bad she couldn't ask the other creatures in the garden about Daisy's whereabouts. What remained was to use indirections to find directions out.

She added two dashes of crushed star anise to the brew.

Marcellus crossed his arms over his chest. "So this... whatever you're doing... is supposed to help us find Daisy?" Despite having settled into cottage life with ease, even enthusiasm, watching Ophelia do something overtly witchy evidently made him twitch.

"Yes. Hush."

She leaned over the steaming mixture, trying to sense its energy. It was so much easier when a recipe called for three and a half petals of wolfsbane and seventy-two seconds of stirring. Nothing was distinct in this made-up recipe.

"Drat!" she said under her breath.

"Maybe we should leave you alone," Barnardo said, turning to go.

"It's all right. You can stay if you want to, but don't distract me." She held out a hand. "Poppy seed."

"Just one?" Marcellus asked, perplexed.

"Just one."

"Okay..." There was a tiny clink as he removed the bottle from the shelf, the hollow sound of a cork being pulled out, and the hushed noise of intaken air as Marcellus held his breath.

Ophelia glanced at her palm. Poppy seeds were too small to feel. Marcellus rolled the seed carefully into her hand, and she plunked it in the potion. Hopefully it wouldn't need to be dry to work.

"*A victory is twice itself when the achiever brings home full numbers,*" she whispered with her face wreathed in warm steam. The meter in that line wasn't as regular as she or the potions normally liked, but the meaning came close to what she wanted.

She stirred three more times and paused.

Silence fell.

"Is that... is it done?" Marcellus asked quietly.

"How should I know?" Ophelia drew the ladle from the liquid.

The potion smelled like earthy tea. Ophelia quite liked it, but she couldn't fully enjoy the sensation when she didn't know if the brew was anything *more*.

"Time to try it out." She wafted the steam around the room (it had grown too hot to bottle for now) and closed her eyes. *Daisy. Daisy. Where's Daisy?*

No picture appeared in her mind. No force tugged her in the right direction. There was only black behind her lids and a question mark in her mind where answers should be.

"Can you tell us where Daisy is?"

Ophelia's eyes snapped open.

Barnardo had asked the question of the potion. In the cauldron, the mixture gave an extra bubble.

"It's not working," she explained, disheartened. Magic was supposed to be her specialty, but it was failing her. If they'd asked her to create illusions of cloud-capped towers or curse someone with pinches all over their skin like honeycomb (a cousin of the metal-black potion), she could have done it. Retrospect didn't help find Daisy now, though. The knowledge made her cranky. "I guess we should split up and see if we can find her," she said.

Marcellus held up a hesitant finger. "Or we could ask the other potions." His voice rose into a question at the end of the sentence.

The unexpected suggestion made Ophelia smile. "That's not a bad idea, Marcellus. I'll ask them. You look."

Barnardo nodded and struck off in search of the wayward hedgehog with Marcellus at his heels.

Ophelia strode to the kitchen, her clothes smelling of anise and dandelion and tea. She stood before the cluster of potion bottles and placed her hands on her hips. "You'd better not have been hiding anything from me about Daisy's whereabouts," she said.

Potions spoke softly, so she had to pay attention to hear them. In the quiet of the cottage, they sometimes seemed loud, but not now, when her worries clambered noisily, saying unhelpful things like, "What if Daisy's dead somewhere? What if she's trapped in that collapsed hole? What if she escaped the bunker somehow and is withering in the toxic air outside?"

Ophelia shook her fluffy hair to clear her mind.

"Daisy?" said the metal-black potion. "Is that the poky rodent?"

Ophelia shushed it. The metal-black potion liked curses and complaining too much to be of any help.

"I heard," said the wispy red potion hurriedly, "that Daisy ran off and married the badger. I told her not to..."

Ophelia rolled her eyes.

A potion in the back puffed out some sparkles, probably because of the excitement of having Ophelia's direct attention.

"Yes?" she prompted.

"Hedgehog," it said, very quietly.

"What's that?" Ophelia moved some of the other bottles to see which one had spoken this time.

She found a squat round bottle, beautiful in its way, with sparkly green liquid inside. It was good for sealing things. She'd told Marcellus about its power once, soon after he arrived. Now, half the liquid was gone. For some reason, Ophelia wasn't cross about that. If anything, she felt pleased.

"Yes?" she prompted again.

"Hedgehog. I saw hedgehog."

"When? Where?"

But the sealing potion offered no other information.

Apparent through the kitchen window, Marcellus and

Barnardo's quest to find Daisy continued. Where else could they look?

Ophelia inwardly groaned. They hadn't thought to check the cottage! Sometimes Daisy crept in there to snuggle into a chair for a nap. (Ophelia and Daisy had certain things in common.)

"Daisy!" she called, although she didn't know if the hedgehog would respond to her name. Treats fared better to summon her. "Where are you?"

She passed through the kitchen toward her favorite armchair, laid thick with fluffy blankets. After digging through the folds and finding no Daisy, she moved on. The bedroom? With the door closed, it was unlikely that she'd gotten in there, but Ophelia checked anyway. She did the same with the library, the bathroom with its big claw-footed tub, the men's bedroom, and half a dozen little alcoves or rooms or recesses that she'd made purely for her own amusement.

No Daisy.

Then she heard a panicked squeak.

Ophelia's heart jolted in her chest as she swiveled toward the noise. It sounded like it had come from the cauldron room.

CHAPTER 4

apologies

I gnoring the irony of it all, Ophelia rushed back to the room where her day had started. She knew that squeak. It was the sound Daisy made when she was startled. It was a common noise.

Rounding the corner, Ophelia found Daisy floating a few inches above the bubbling cauldron. The hedgehog's little legs flailed in the air, but her efforts did nothing to help her predicament. Instead, she slowly rotated like a balloon. Her small black eyes, wide with terror, finally landed on Ophelia in a cry for help.

"Oh dear!" Ophelia exclaimed, gingerly holding out cupped hands.

Daisy continued to ascend.

"What did you do?" Ophelia's fingers carefully closed around Daisy's little body. Once she held the hedgehog securely against her middle, Ophelia looked toward the door. "I found her!"

Marcellus showed up so quickly he must have been

inside the cottage already. Barnardo appeared a few seconds later. They stared at Daisy, who was still breathing hard, trying to calm down.

"I found her floating in here," Ophelia explained.

Marcellus's smile faltered. "Floating? You mean, in the…" He gestured toward the potion.

"No, no. In the air. She must have drunk some of the potion."

"It makes people fly? But I thought…"

"Not people. But hedgehogs, evidently."

Barnardo raised an eyebrow at Ophelia. Maybe he could tell she was guessing about the limits of the potion's power.

"Wow…" Marcellus wiped his forehead, gazing in wonder at the brew, the hedgehog, and Ophelia.

"The important thing is that she's safe," Ophelia said.

As if to punctuate the statement, Daisy hiccupped. Her frantic heartbeat had begun to slow.

Ophelia drew her up against her cheek. Daisy's spikes poked lightly against her face. The sensation didn't hurt, and it was so good to have Daisy back that Ophelia wouldn't have minded if it did. "Was it yummy? Did you think it was tea?"

Daisy wiggled her nose.

"It does smell like tea," Barnardo commented seriously.

"I'm glad she's okay," said Marcellus.

Ophelia briefly considered disposing of the makeshift mixture in the cauldron, but the power to make things float was very interesting. She'd try it again on something non-living.

"You've had quite a fright," Ophelia cooed to Daisy, who gave a wee sigh of agreement.

"Oh!" Marcellus straightened like a soldier with news. His pale face grew a shade paler. "I think I figured out what destroyed the burrow."

"What was it?" Ophelia asked.

"It caved in because I was..." He dropped his eyes, and his immaculate posture began to deflate. "I was watering the trees on that side and didn't see it there. I think I flooded it and then it got all trampled when I adjusted the bat house."

His grimace was so cartoonish it almost made Ophelia laugh, if she hadn't been so indignant on Daisy's behalf.

"I didn't know that's where it was until I saw you over there today." He kicked the ground.

"Apologize," Ophelia demanded.

"What?"

"Apologize to Daisy."

"But..."

Ophelia fixed him with a glare. Barnardo patted him on the shoulder, urging him forward. The men didn't object to all her animals, but it was a rarity for anyone to have pets on the outside, since they used up precious resources. They probably hadn't encountered many cute fuzzy creatures before stumbling on her oasis.

Marcellus looked sheepish. "I'm sorry, Daisy," he muttered, awkward but sincere. "I didn't mean to destroy your home."

Ophelia held the hedgehog out so she could sniff

Marcellus's face, which she did rigorously as if smelling for repentance.

"She accepts your apology," said Ophelia, drawing Daisy back.

Marcellus sighed.

"And since you have experience building animal homes now, you can help her find a new home too."

"That was for the bats," Marcellus protested.

Ophelia shrugged. "Can't be helped. Our little Daisy needs a safe place to live where she can't get into things that don't concern her." For this last statement, Ophelia lifted the hedgehog so they could look each other in the eye.

"Just tell us what to do," said Barnardo. "Daisy's a decent sort of hedgehog."

Ophelia could tell Barnardo was trying to be sweet, which wasn't often a stretch for him, but he acted at a loss when confronted with a homeless hedgehog. His seriousness made Ophelia clamp down her teeth to keep from smiling.

"She is. It's all right, Marcellus. Daisy is safe and sound. I'll show you the other homes and burrows in case you haven't found them yet."

Marcellus nodded.

"Good." Daisy in hand, Ophelia swept from the room. "Time for apple muffins, I think."

She'd made some the day before and, miraculously, there were still leftovers.

Daisy perked up right away. Her tiny claws scraped against Ophelia's fingers as she tried to wiggle out of her grip toward the muffins.

"One muffin," Ophelia instructed, pointing a stern finger at the eager hedgehog. "Only one." Convinced Daisy hadn't heard a word through the haze of apple muffin excitement, Ophelia set her down on the table. To her surprise, Daisy ran toward the muffin she presented like an astronaut would run on the moon, bouncing and floating before touching down again. She seemed to be in no danger of rising all the way to the ceiling, so Ophelia merely watched as Daisy collided with her treat, making happy squeaking noises.

Ophelia's gaze shifted to the collection of potions on the counter. The plump green sealant had been right. A hedgehog had run past. She winked at the bottle, which released another glittery puff.

"She loves that," said Marcellus, picking up the four remaining muffins and taking them out of reach.

Barnardo snagged one as the plate passed him on the way to a high shelf.

"Thank you for your help today," Ophelia said to Marcellus. "The potions did know what had happened to Daisy. I just didn't know how to listen. And coming clean about destroying the burrow..." She cleared her throat to shove down any negative feelings that still lingered. Marcellus hadn't meant any harm. "I appreciate that you were honest."

"Of course," he replied easily.

Something loosened inside her. Maybe it was the fact that she could fully be herself—powers and all—and Marcellus could be himself, even with mistakes. Those small doors that everyone kept closed inside themselves didn't need to stay that way, not around Marcellus and Barnardo.

She smiled. The noises of Daisy happily munching her consolation muffin filled the cramped room.

"We can seal the walls of the burrow this time so it can't collapse," she said. "Maybe add a nest."

Everyone, from the hedgehog to the potions to the humans, heartily endorsed that idea and set to work as soon as Daisy finished eating. Their spiny friend deserved a comfortable rest after such an eventful day.

yuletide magic

CHAPTER 1

sliding

The roof of Ophelia's cottage was very slippery. It didn't look like it from below, with all those bumpy shingles. The surface didn't angle down like an ordinary pitched roof, but rather rolled like hills or waves. Despite all that, when Ophelia, Barnardo, and Marcellus decided to climb up there in order to slide down into the patch of heather and magical snow, the roof felt slipperier than she remembered.

Marcellus breathed into mittened hands. "How did you make it this cold, Ophelia?"

Ophelia struggled step by tiny step to reach the highest point of the roof. Answering his question at the same time would break her concentration. She paused. "I performed a puppet show for the amplifier," she confessed. "It was very amused."

Evidently, so was Marcellus, because his mouth turned down at the edges like he was trying not to laugh. He climbed a few more paces toward where Barnardo waited for them.

"You try getting that potion to work when you don't flatter it," grumbled Ophelia, taking another miniature step.

Snow fell softly around them, but she hadn't managed to perform the same feat over the garden. Sparkling flakes floated around the cottage, but not beyond, as if one snowy, house-sized cloud stopped just above. Like they lived in a shaken snow globe.

The puppet show, as humiliating as it was (the potions kept coming up with terrible story suggestions that the amplifier insisted she perform), was worth it. Neither the bunker with her lovely world inside nor the wasted world outside had natural seasons anymore. Last she heard, the outside world had a vaguely cooler season to break up the toxic, dry norm. But Ophelia remembered seasons and loved them. Some of her favorite books were picture books depicting forests and gardens at each stage of life. In the cozy library, she had one opened to a page showing full-color illustrations of a maple tree in spring, summer, autumn, and winter. On its makeshift stand, it took up half a shelf.

"Do you want help, Ophelia?" Barnardo asked, reaching down with a rough hand.

"No, thank you," she said primly and heaved herself up the rest of the way. Before Barnardo and Marcellus arrived, she'd slid down the roof on days when she wanted excitement, and she had scrambled to the top by herself, thank you very much.

The three of them sat on the crest of the roof, facing the heather. From here, the garden looked like a small, tangled wonderland fairies could get lost in. The apple tree stood proudly just down a garden lane from the beehive. There went Polonius the badger along the path, probably thinking something like, "Those foolish humans. One day they'll break their necks and they'll have no one to blame but themselves."

"Ready?" said Ophelia. "One, two, THREE!"

They dislodged themselves and glided down the slippery roof. A slip, a slide, one spot where they banked left, and then...

Open air.

Thump!

They landed in the thick, snowy heather, breathless and laughing.

"That's wonderful!" Marcellus exclaimed, throwing up his hands before reaching for the roof's edge again. He'd crocheted new gloves for himself, using (as he'd gleefully explained several times) an adjusted engine coolant auxiliary return hose for a crochet hook. The gloves were actually his second project. The first was a lumpy patch to mend a hole in his shirt. Once he made that uneven square of crocheted fabric, he became utterly obsessed. The gloves, gray because they came from yarn made from Gertrude the rabbit's excess fluff, fit Marcellus well.

"One more," Ophelia conceded. Her skirt had grown cold and wet from the snow, and she looked forward to relaxing inside. Before they'd gone out, she'd popped a pot of water on the stove along with round orange slices and clove buds so the cottage would smell festive when they entered. The three of them had reached a natural stopping point in Yule decorating and felt stiff. Hence, the snowy roof sliding.

Barnardo hauled himself up the lip of the uneven roof after Marcellus. Around his shoulders fluttered a sparrow who had taken a shine to him the past few weeks. At this point, the bird was practically Barnardo's pet. Unfortunately, he hadn't named it anything interesting or endearing. When Ophelia asked what he planned to call the sparrow, he simply shrugged, gave the bird a covert, twinkling look of friendship, and said, "Bird."

Bird hopped after Barnardo up the roof, making tiny, spiky impressions in the snow. Behind him climbed Ophelia. She counted her small steps up, which turned into counting the tasks still to do for Yuletide (there were many), which turned into adding more ideas to the celebration, which turned into re-counting.

"Careful, Ophelia," said Marcellus, who craned his neck to look back.

As if she needed someone to remind her. He'd only lived here for six and a half months. She'd been climbing the cottage far longer than that.

She went back to counting. Snow fell around her. The hypnotic sound of Barnardo's boots crunching in front of her and the twittering song of Bird blended with the numbers in her head.

And then... oop! Her foot slipped. She clambered for a handhold, but all the shingles were smooth or angled the wrong way. She bumped un-gracefully down to the leftward tilting part, then flung—*umph!*—backward off the roof.

For a second, she lay sprawled on the ground, only halfway on the soft heather. A piercing ache shot from her ankle all the way up her leg. Groaning, she tensed, heather pressed against her cheek.

"Ophelia!" Marcellus called.

Someone landed with a thud beside her. She saw only his brown boots. "Are you all right?" Barnardo asked.

"Mmm," she said, although she'd meant to say, "Yes, perfectly."

"Let's get you inside. You might have sprained something."

Another thump and Marcellus landed beside Barnardo, who scooped her in his arms.

"Hey!" she cried.

"Do you want to walk instead?" Barnardo asked kindly, but as if he knew the answer.

She flopped her head back. "No."

It was actually far more comfortable to be carried than she would have guessed. Barnardo was strong and took care not to knock her painful ankle against any doorframes. He tracked mud through the cottage, but that couldn't be helped. The warm kitchen did smell nice, but at the scent of orange and clove, the list of Yule preparations yet to do filled her head again and a small surge of panic threaded through her. She winced.

"Just try to lie still," said Barnardo, kicking open her bedroom door and setting her down.

"I don't want to lie still."

"Trust me, your ankle says differently."

From over Barnardo's shoulder, Marcellus raised an eyebrow at her as if to say, "He gets like this." And also, "He's right."

She pursed her lips. Barnardo and Marcellus weren't in the habit of treating her like some fragile thing—thank goodness!—and she'd always assumed they'd seen some combat, since they arrived at her door wearing washed-out military uniforms. They didn't talk about it. But that meant, as much as she hated to admit it, Barnardo probably did know what he was talking about.

She blew a strand of unruly hair out of her face.

Just in time for Yuletide.

CHAPTER 2

Soup

Ophelia expected lying in bed to be dreadful since there was so much to be done, and so much she was missing by being cooped in that room. Yuletide snow fell outside the windows, orange and clove boiled in the kitchen, and half-finished decorations littered nearly every room.

But, as much as she hated to admit it, her situation wasn't nearly as dreadful as she'd thought. The discrepancy between expectation and reality left her unjustly grumpy.

She frowned at Barnardo as he took the long scarf that had been hanging from a lampshade in the cauldron room from Marcellus, and lifted Ophelia's foot in the other hand.

"I was a medic in the army," Barnardo explained.

"You were?" Ophelia tried not to feel self-conscious as he began wrapping the injured ankle. Barnardo had needed to help her take her boot and thick sock off.

A moment of hesitation passed, and then he added, "By necessity."

Marcellus left Barnardo to tend to her injury. Hopefully he was taking the boiling water off the stove.

"What terrible timing!" Ophelia lamented. "Right before the Yule celebration!" She was seconds away from crossing her arms like an angry child. She never got hurt—at least, nothing serious.

She'd cut herself while chopping carrots last year. Eight months ago, she'd somehow gotten a cold. A spot of tea had cured her right away. But a turned ankle? Never in the history of roof sliding had she made such a grave and obvious mistake.

The scarf went over and around, over and around.

"I can do that," she said, stretching to take the length of cloth from him.

He leaned out of her reach. "Lie back," he instructed.

"I don't want you to do this for me."

"You've done plenty for us."

She didn't have an answer for that, so she did as he said. Faintly, on the other side of the door, she could hear Bird tweeting, followed by an old record turning on the phonograph. Marcellus must have turned it on.

That reminded her—she hadn't finished gifts for Marcellus or Barnardo! That was a travesty. She gritted her teeth. This injury really did have the worst timing.

Barnardo finished winding the cloth and set her foot down on a fluffy blanket. "Better?"

She tried pointing her toe. The binding prevented her from doing anything more than flexing her ankle the tiniest bit, but that was enough to send shooting pain across the joint. "Maybe."

Barnardo straightened.

"Yule is ruined. We never should have climbed on the roof," Ophelia grumbled.

"You don't believe either of those things."

Barnardo's voice had a way of soothing her, and it did so again now. That didn't mean she didn't want to grumble some more.

"Will you finish the projects we started?" she asked. By the time she stopped counting, there were nineteen pieces of preparation to be done.

"Don't worry about that. Do you need anything else?"

Barnardo's pale blue eyes were kind, but she felt like a child when he asked that question, and she didn't enjoy feeling helpless. She'd made this cottage, this garden, this life all on her own. She took care of the plants, the animals, the magic, and the people here. No one took care of her.

"No," she answered stubbornly, considering making a list of holiday preparations with little asterisks next to the items she could do in bed.

Barnardo's lips stretched in a rueful smile.

"I'm fine," she insisted.

The instant Barnardo nodded and turned away, she wished she'd asked for something to do, but she didn't call after him.

He left the door ajar. Outside, "The Fairy on the Christmas Tree" warbled softly.

She sighed. Technically, she felt comfortable. Her room was warm and dry, and the blankets cocooned her. For someone who had just injured an ankle, this was about as good as it could get.

So why did she feel so restless? Even guilty?

"That's silly," she muttered to herself. No need to feel silly for falling off the roof, but telling herself that wasn't helping.

A soft knock came at the door. "Ophelia?" Marcellus stuck his head in. "Want some soup?"

"I haven't made soup."

"I know. I'm about to put some on."

"Oh!" First Barnardo wrapping her ankle and now this. She wanted to protest that she didn't need any of it, but part of her heart told her to be quiet and enjoy. She gave in. "Then yes. I'd love some. And—"

Marcellus turned back.

"And, could you bring the materials for the popcorn garland, and the book with the bells on the spine from the library? It's on the left when you walk in, about halfway up." She clasped her hands together.

Marcellus smiled. "Sure. Soup, popcorn, book. Got it!" He bustled away to get the soup started.

Ophelia had never had qualms about enjoying the garden or doing little things for fun. Before the men arrived, she'd dress up or talk to the animals. Once, she made a potion whose only purpose was to change her voice so it sounded silly and high for a few minutes. Nothing about her lovely life made her cringe with the shame of thinking she should have less. Until this moment. Apparently, deep inside, there remained a shard of independence that pierced deep. Life was friendship too, wasn't it? And friendship meant being helped as much as it meant helping.

Of course, she had to become helpless at Yuletide, when

nights were darkest but the promise of light still shone bright.

Ophelia cleared her throat. She was getting sentimental.

Marcellus brought her the book and the popcorn and, eventually, a bowl of onion soup, complete with bread and cheese on top. He handed it to her with special ceremony. She took it from him gravely and took a sip from the spoon. Marcellus's eyes sparkled as he watched her.

"Mmm," she said.

"Good," said Marcellus, who looked relieved.

"You should make this again."

"Maybe I will. Barnardo said it should heal you right up."

Her mouth twisted in a half-smile. She still couldn't prepare for Yule like she'd intended, but the soup definitely helped. Barnardo was right. In a moment she'd go back to wondering about decorations, but for now the soup tasted heavenly, salty and savory. She downed another mouthful of the brown broth. "Thank you, Marcellus."

He nodded and left.

Ophelia ate her soup alone. Her concentration wavered when she picked up the book. She only threaded a few pieces of popcorn.

When she woke up today, she decided she would not be sad or worried. It would be a joyful day, a perfect Yule celebration. And it had been, until the incident on the roof.

Now, she had too much time to remember back to another Yuletide, years ago, when she'd found a bunker in the middle of the longest night of the year and prepared to build a cottage.

CHAPTER 3

friends

Ophelia's room smelled like onion soup, blankets surrounded her, and she had a naughty book disguised as a different story sitting on the end table. She should have been happy. But she kept noticing how alone she was.

The fact didn't bother her all those years while she built a life for herself, did it? She didn't think so. But now that she'd found friends—family, really—and holiday cheer went on somewhere else, out of sight, her stomach twisted.

I will not call out like a child. She balled her fists. This was ridiculous. A twisted ankle meant she had to rest, no matter what Yule decorating and baking and gift-making she wanted to do. She sat a few minutes longer.

"Harumph," Polonius the badger would say. "No reason to whine."

"But, my dear sir," she'd reply, "I'm..."

Lonely.

No, she couldn't say it.

She tried dozing for a few minutes, listening to the crackly tunes floating in from the phonograph. That was better. Not perfect, but better.

When a knock came at the door, she bolted upright. The movement made her wince. Who knew that motion was enough to upset her ankle?

"Yes?" she called. "Come in!"

It was Barnardo. "Comfy?" he asked.

"I want to be moved to the room near the kitchen," she blurted.

His eyebrows rose. "Are you sure? I don't want to move you if I don't have to." He cast a meaningful look at her wrapped foot.

"Please."

"If you're worried about all the Yule preparations, you don't need to worry. Marcellus and I don't care if—"

"I do." She pushed herself to the edge of the bed.

Barnardo flew to her side. "Woah! Okay, I'll bring you out."

"I don't have presents. I was going to gather all these ingredients..." She felt like a different person as all these confessions poured out.

Barnardo gave a soft smile of understanding. "I'll bring you out."

"I think I can walk."

"Ophelia."

"With your help."

He sat beside her, allowing her to wrap one arm around his neck. They stood together, while she only put weight on one foot. She hopped slowly out of the room.

"Barnardo!" Marcellus cried indignantly from where he sat hunched in a focused posture in the armchair. He placed an awkward elbow in front of his project to hide it, but the big crochet hook in his hand gave his secret away. Marcellus scowled.

Ophelia laughed. "What's that?"

"Nothing. Barnardo, keep going! What is she doing out of the room?"

"*She* was tired of being cooped up," Ophelia answered. She heard how ironic that sounded once it was out of her mouth. Her cottage and garden never felt stifling, though. She had everything she needed.

"Don't look," Marcellus pleaded.

Barnardo said nothing but nudged her to hop past Marcellus toward the kitchen. Straight ahead sat a one-armed sofa. They maneuvered around the phonograph and a pile of fabric rings constructed of dyed airship material. She'd pictured making it into a garland to drape the stove.

Listening, she noted that the pot of water had been taken off the heat. That lovely citrus clove smell still rose faintly above the new onion scent, though.

"Do you know what Marcellus is making?" Ophelia whispered.

"I haven't looked."

She rolled her eyes. Barnardo needed to be nosier sometimes.

"Here," he said, easing her down. "Is this what you wanted?"

From the sofa, Ophelia could see into the kitchen and two other areas. "Good," she said with a nod.

"I was in the middle of making that garland," he explained, "but your stubbornness about the ankle worried me."

Ophelia frowned. "Stubbornness?"

He looked back at her stoically.

"Fine, yes," she conceded. "It's nicer out here."

"Where do you want the garland?" he asked, gesturing toward the pile of interconnected rings. "I know you wanted Yule to be nice and decorated."

"I do." She pursed her lips, considering a new place. Perhaps the stove wasn't the wisest choice. "There." She pointed to a corner of the room that didn't have lights or holly or bells or faux velvet.

From the kitchen, she heard the faintest rustle of the potions reacting to her choice. Several were not in favor. The wispy red potion wanted the garland right overhead. That position would place the garland over the sink, a terrible option. Ophelia didn't bother to respond.

"I thought... maybe outside," Barnardo suggested.

At first, Ophelia didn't understand what he was talking about. The fabric rings, because they'd once been part of an operational airship, had weather-proof coating to protect them from her enchanted snow. But why outside?

"For Bird?" Ophelia guessed.

Barnardo's cheeks darkened. "And the others." She could barely hear his murmur.

Her heart warmed. That corner could be bare for now. "Outside it is."

Ophelia could imagine Daisy the hedgehog exclaiming with joy when she saw the rings festooned in the garden.

"Harumph," Polonius would snort, while secretly loving it.

Gertrude the rabbit and Fortinbras the horny toad rarely chimed into such conversations, but she suspected they'd enjoy some Yuletide cheer too.

Eventually, Marcellus returned from whatever not-so-secret project he was working on. Ophelia happily directed the two of them to complete many of the preparations that had plagued her mind.

Her ankle twinged when she sat up too violently or shifted her position on the couch, but that didn't matter anymore. What an unexpected joy not to have to do everything herself. Having help for six months hadn't given her completely new expectations. She *liked* doing things herself. But, it turned out, she liked having caring friends even more, who could step in when she wasn't able to. This Yule wasn't like that day years ago when she opened a heavy door, lifted her chin, and set to work.

Peace settled heavy.

But I don't have presents for them. That was the last thought before Ophelia's eyes closed and she fell asleep.

CHAPTER 4

gifts

"**D**o you have a match?"

"No, do you? Oops!"

"Marcellus! Ophelia's sleeping!"

Ophelia rolled over on the sofa. Her bound ankle sent shocks through her leg in protest. When she opened her eyes, Marcellus and Barnardo were visible through the kitchen doorway. Marcellus held a stack of paper snowflakes in his hand. Barnardo stood on a ladder, hanging them from the ceiling. Ophelia wasn't sure what had caused the crash, but she suspected the candlestick overturned into a plate of cookies.

"I'm not asleep anymore," she said. "Are those cookies?"

"Gingerbread," Marcellus declared proudly, righting the candlestick. "They were supposed to be little men."

Barnardo's lips flattened a little. Apparently, that design didn't turn out properly.

"How long have I slept?"

"Not long," Barnardo answered.

Ophelia rubbed sleep from her eyes. Around her, the cottage had transformed. Nothing magical, of course, since she hadn't been able to help with most of it, but the holiday cheer felt like magic to her. Faint music kept its beat through the phonograph. There were ribbons and berries and paper stars, garlands and lanterns rearranged around the cottage. Snowflakes hung in the kitchen. Miniature stockings dangled above the fireplace. Those must have been for the animals.

The longer she looked, the more emotion swelled up. "You didn't have to do all this," she croaked.

"Oh yes we did!" Marcellus declared. "Yule wouldn't be the same otherwise. Isn't that what you said?"

"I don't think so," she muttered.

"Something like that," Barnardo said, attaching another snowflake to the ceiling.

"We thought you'd like it." Marcellus gave her a wide, eager smile.

The two of them were making her feel more and more. "I do," she grouched. Then a memory returned to her. "Oh!"

"What?"

"In the cauldron room, in a cupboard near the floor…" She gave instructions for how to find a collection of not-presents for everyone to set around the table. They weren't her first choice to give to people who had become so dear to her, but they were something. Marcellus ran to fetch them.

"These?" he asked when he returned. In his palms he cupped three cylinders wrapped neatly with red paper that flared at the ends.

"Those," she confirmed.

Barnardo stepped down off the ladder. "That's it, I think. Unless you wanted a little more, Ophelia?" He leaned so she could see more of him through the doorway.

"Please say no," Marcellus cut in. "I'm ready to eat."

She laughed, unable to help herself. "No. It looks perfect!" She'd almost forgotten how much could get done without magic. "Time to eat, I guess."

Marcellus beamed. When Barnardo came to fetch her and bring her to a chair at the table, Marcellus gave a little bow and said in a grand voice, "For your pleasure this evening I have made squash stew, curried eggs with mustard, and sage bread. Oh, and blood orange toddies with honey."

Barnardo carried Ophelia past him.

"Barnardo did most of the decorating," he admitted.

"Sounds like you did all of the cooking," she exclaimed, inhaling the delicious scent in the kitchen. It made her feel weak with delight.

Just when she thought her enjoyment couldn't grow any more, she gaped at the table, which she'd only partially been able to see from the sofa where she lay swathed in blankets. Each seat had one of the magical crackers that Ophelia had made Marcellus fetch from the cauldron room, along with a sloppily wrapped package and little card. On one end lay the plate of misshapen cookies, all the limbs twisting together in one gingery mass.

"Thank you," she said, eyes welling.

The metal-black potion murmured something rude about how she needed to pull herself together.

Barnardo arranged her in a seat at the table. Marcellus bustled around, scooping out plates of food and presenting them proudly. At last, he sat too, barely able to contain his excitement.

The food did taste scrumptious. The squash stew looked a little muddy and there were big chunks of sage leaves woven throughout the bread, but the flavor made up for those missteps.

For a while, they didn't talk. All their focus centered on the meal. When Ophelia's attention finally surfaced, Daisy the hedgehog looked in at the window with Bird perched at her side. They watched the three humans eat with glowing attentiveness, waiting for any morsel to fall. Daisy had gotten bolder since the men arrived, evidently.

"All right," Ophelia declared, wiping her hands of crumbs. Bird promptly swooped into the kitchen with brazenness that would have made Polonius splutter in horror. "Time for holiday crackers! I made these a couple years ago for myself and forgot all about them until today." She only had a vague memory of what she'd put inside. Magical things, she recalled, including enchanted fortunes, but beyond that she hardly knew what to expect.

"I haven't seen one of these since I was a boy," Barnardo said, picking up the one beside his plate.

"Are they presents?" Marcellus asked.

"Of a sort," Ophelia answered. "You go first. Pull it open."

A line deepened between his eyebrows, but he followed her instruction.

Pop!

Daisy squeaked and ran for cover. A ribbon of smoke wreathed up from the husk of the opened cracker.

"Is it supposed to do that?" Marcellus asked urgently.

But Barnardo was laughing, and that was answer enough.

Cautiously, Marcellus pulled apart the pieces and tipped out what lay inside: something flat and shiny like paper folded lengthwise, a cloudy marble, and a tiny metal figurine of the historical Ophelia after whom she was named wearing a dress and holding an armful of flowers. Marcellus teased open the shiny paper. It unfolded into a crown just big enough to slot over his head.

"Try it on!" Ophelia urged.

Dubiously, he donned the crown. Then he picked up the marble to inspect it more closely. "What's this?"

"A fortune," she said. "Here, let me activate it." She took it from him as several potions murmured from the corner in surprise. Ophelia had been reckless with her magic early on. She had never conserved it, though she'd been taught to do so. She had one life, and was dealt a challenging hand, and wanted to live and experience as much as she could, even if it meant creating silly little fortunes in holiday crackers to bring herself some joy.

"Go thou forth;" she chanted.

"And fortune play upon thy prosperous helm,
As thy auspicious mistress!"

Inside the marble, clouds began to churn and rotate. Marcellus's eyes rounded. Barnardo leaned in. A faint, whispering voice that sounded much like her own filled the air around them. "To repair a heart, repair a home," it said.

Marcellus scrunched his mouth to the side, evidently moved by the simple message.

"Your turn." Ophelia repeated the same steps with Barnardo's marble, once he popped his holiday cracker. Instead of a figurine of the original Ophelia, Barnardo found an ornament shaped like a jewel.

Again came the voice—her own voice—ghosting over the table. "See the future as a horizon, not a mirror."

Barnardo raised his eyebrows. Ophelia had no reply. She hadn't magicked these fortunes to say anything in particular, just something nice and true.

The final cracker exploded like a mini firework when Ophelia pulled it open. A third paper crown, a set of small bells, and the marble. She said the words with the strong meter spells enjoyed, and the final fortune spoke. "Better than magic is the love of a friend."

"Hm," she said, wrestling the crown over her curls.

"The crackers were a success," Barnardo concluded, digging into his wrapped present.

"That's...!" Marcellus held out a hand but drew it back again.

Inside the wrapping lay a lumpy, folded sweater. When Barnardo held it up, a large letter B made of thick, uneven lines filled the front.

Ophelia giggled.

"I thought maybe you would enjoy something like..." Marcellus began.

Barnardo struggled to keep his expression even. "It's very thoughtful."

Marcellus sighed with relief and tossed a smile at Ophelia. When Marcellus turned away from him, Barnardo's glass-blue eyes fanned with apprehension around the edges.

Ophelia hid her smirk and opened her own gift.

A crocheted airship as big as her forearm.

"It's wonderful!" she exclaimed and meant it.

"Really?" Marcellus looked younger when he felt uncertain.

"Yes." She held it up as though it were flying through the air. "It will go marvelously in the library."

"Yes! That's... that's great. I'll help you hang it."

Finally, they opened their cards from Barnardo. The sentiments were short, but both Marcellus and Ophelia found themselves wiping their eyes after reading.

"Not a ruined Yule, I hope," Barnardo said in his soothing way, pouring everyone another round of toddies.

"Not ruined at all," Ophelia replied. Truthfully, she'd forgotten all about the incident with her ankle the past few minutes. Her thoughts were taken up with paper crowns, good food, and even better friends.

"I found this place six years ago, you know," she added. "To the day."

Marcellus mouthed his surprise.

"It was dark," she went on, "but there was nothing to do but make the most of it. This Yule... is much better."

Barnardo leaned over and gently squeezed her hand.

"Yes," she said, banishing the lump in her throat. "Who's for dessert?"

Marcellus beamed and reached for the plate of cookies, breaking off three pieces before passing them along.

"And we must see that sweater on you, Barnardo." Ophelia smiled cheekily at him.

He regarded the crocheted garment like an unpleasant duty that needed doing.

"You don't have to," Marcellus put in.

"Nonsense!" Ophelia snapped. "Go change."

Barnardo exhaled, scooped up the lumpy sweater with a grim smile, and left. "Yes, your majesty."

Ophelia and Marcellus downed cookies at an alarming rate, considering Barnardo was only gone perhaps eighty seconds.

He emerged, arms wide to demonstrate the sweater. It was gray, like Gertrude the rabbit, except for the B in the center, which had been dyed blue. The sleeves were too short and the size too big. The overall impression was of fluffiness.

"I think it's perfect," Ophelia said.

"I almost got the sleeves right," Marcellus added with a grimace.

Barnardo tried to pull them down to his wrists. His golden crown was nowhere to be seen.

"Very cozy," Ophelia said. "And you just started crocheting. I think it's impressive."

Marcellus reddened.

"Is it comfortable?" she prompted.

"It is," Barnardo confirmed.

"Well then. Marcellus and I will eat all the cookies if you don't sit down and join us again." She bit back a chuckle.

"You're very demanding," Barnardo said, but he sat. A joke twinkled in his eye.

How much had changed in six years. Her lovely cottage represented a place where life paused, she had thought. Nothing would change unless she changed it. Now, there were two others who could celebrate and relax and adventure with her. That faraway Yule night really was the darkest in her life. With Marcellus, Barnardo, and her animal companions, there was variety, spice. There was joy —the perfect complement to their Yuletide celebration together.

roque spells

CHAPTER 1

picnic

W hen Ophelia had declared this the perfect day for a picnic, she hadn't counted on poky grass.

Of course, every day was essentially the same in the bunker where her cottage and garden sprawled alive and chaotic and beautiful. The weather never changed unless she changed it. The string lights above the garden path provided most of the light.

To be fair, the picnic was lovely—apple muffins (Daisy the hedgehog's favorite!), raspberry scones with cream, quiche with dried tomatoes, leeks, spinach, and sharp cheese, and cups of hearty black tea for all. Now they sprawled on the blanket, hazy with good food.

The big pillow Ophelia leaned against wasn't large enough to stave off creeping tendrils of plants and blades of grass. Cool greenery tickled the tiny sliver of bare back between her oversized sweater and long patchy skirt. Lips flattening, she adjusted her skirt. At least the blanket they'd laid out in the garden could fit them all: Ophelia, Marcellus, and Barnardo.

Ophelia turned a page in her book, but her focus had broken. The adventures of seafaring women pirates (usually one of her very favorites) suddenly lost the thread. Across from her sat Marcellus crocheting something gray and suspiciously hat-shaped with his enormous makeshift crochet needle. Next to him, Barnardo wrote in a tiny notebook. Bird sat on his shoulder, as if reading. Ophelia suspected the book was a journal of his thoughts and feelings, but he never discussed his writing. Maybe it was stories about seafaring women pirates. A smile curled the edge of her mouth at the thought. If that were true, she would steal that little book if she had to.

Marcellus stretched, spooking Bird, who had apparently forgotten all about him. Bird settled next to Barnardo again, but not before leveling a beady glance at Marcellus.

"I'll bring this in," Marcellus declared, standing and taking the picnic basket and three teacups with him. He left behind the half-finished hat.

"Thank you!" Ophelia called after him as he tromped down the path back to the cottage. She turned to her attention to Barnardo. "What are you writing?"

She knew it broke the unspoken code to give him his privacy regarding the notebook, but her curiosity got the better of her.

He gave her a look that resembled Bird's expression toward Marcellus a moment ago, except without the angry intentions. "I didn't ask what you were reading."

She flourished her book. "It's the story of Adara, the most feared pirate on the seven seas. She fights sea monsters and bandits. Once, she hides aboard a merchant ship filled with coffee for two weeks. It's very exciting."

"I'm sure she was excited too, after two weeks and nothing but coffee," Barnardo laughed.

"It's true. I—"

"Ophelia!" Marcellus's panicked voice cut through their conversation like a knife through a strawberry.

Ophelia and Barnardo rocketed to their feet.

Marcellus sprinted high-kneed toward them, barely avoiding trampling the peppers. "It's—"

For a few breaths, he didn't say anything else, but that only made Ophelia's heartbeat rise too. "What?" she demanded. "What's wrong?" Instinctively, she scanned for her beloved animals.

There was Daisy the hedgehog, safe and sound but clearly rattled by Marcellus's demeanor. Over there, Polonius the badger peeked around the beehive to criticize them for the noise. Gertrude the rabbit munched basil, unbothered. Even Fortinbras the horny toad made his stiff way over the path. All accounted for, then.

"It's the silverware!"

Ophelia frowned. "The silverware?" It had never been the cause of such alarm before. Yes, it didn't match. One spoon was too big for eating and too small for serving, but Barnardo usually claimed that one so the others didn't have to...

"It's alive!"

Barnardo exhaled audibly. "Marcellus," he said smoothly, "why—"

"It's chopping at the walls! And, I don't know. I didn't know what to do."

Ophelia and Barnardo were already moving toward the cottage. The silverware had never done anything remotely like that before. Strange. What would have made it come alive? Had she left a spell going, or a potion on the stove that wasn't finished?

No, she could be absent-minded, but she'd remember that.

"Get the net," said Barnardo. "Blankets. Anything like that. We'll take care of it." The way he spoke made it sound like he dealt with rogue dishware all the time.

Marcellus gave him a curt nod and rushed ahead of the other two.

Ophelia racked her mind for any spell that could be useful. The metal-black potion would be happy to step in, no doubt, but it was too dangerous to set loose something that was essentially a deadly poison. At best, it would target the violent silverware directly and then they'd be without eating utensils. At worst, all their lives would be at risk. It had muttered something about "that cursed slime, that absolute sheepgut" at supper last night, referring to one of them. Ophelia had shushed it and not asked for clarification.

They reached the door to the cottage too soon. She hadn't come up with one viable solution to use if Barnardo's pragmatic idea fell through. Already, sounds of clinking resounded through the windows, as if a sword fight were happening in the kitchen.

Marcellus grimaced and jumped inside. Determined to unravel this mess and protect her beloved cottage from more harm, Ophelia hiked up her skirt and stalked after him.

CHAPTER 2

silverware

Inside the cottage, Ophelia beheld chaos. Forks fought with knives in midair while spoons attempted to scoop their way to freedom through the walls. A particularly vigorous whisk stirred the pot of soup on the stove into a frothing mess. Potions screamed and muttered feeble things like "no, not the teapot!" and "oh dear, I knew this would happen."

As if the silverware could sense the presence of intruders, its activities grew more frantic. A fork scraped the wall near the doorway where Ophelia stood.

"Ack! Enough of that!" she chided, slamming the door closed and reaching for the enchanted fork. It stabbed at her fingers. "Hey!"

"All right, Ophelia?" asked Marcellus, covering his head with his hands and peering back at her.

"Yes. Where's Barnardo?"

"Here." Barnardo emerged from the hallway, gripping the handle of a spoon. It struggled to get free, whipping his arm this way and that. Barnardo's face was set hard as a rock, but the absurdity of the situation tempted Ophelia to laugh. The fact that the spoon could move even Barnardo's strong arm was cause for concern, though.

Marcellus disappeared through the tunnel-like hall, reappearing seconds later with a fluffy blanket.

"Try it on this one," Barnardo instructed as he attempted to hold out the spoon. "Put the blanket over this."

Marcellus tossed the blanket like a net and covered the thrashing utensil. Barnardo let go, but the spoon continued to float erratically beneath the blanket like some possessed woolen balloon.

"Eek!" Ophelia threw herself at Marcellus just in time to pull him out of the path of an errant knife.

His eyes rounded to perfect circles as his gaze found the blade embedded in the wall.

"This is ridiculous! We can't round them all up with just blankets. It will take too long." She glared at the knife wobbling in her cottage wall. A few centimeters to the side and it would have stabbed a framed illustration of a beautiful ash tree. And that was the better of the two disasters they'd barely avoided. Her eyes narrowed. It was time to take more drastic measures to protect herself, her friends, and her hard-won home. "I'm going to the cauldron room," she shouted as she ran. "Be careful!"

"You too!" Marcellus called after her.

She reached the alcove quickly, passing violent butter knives on the way. One of them scraped across the cover of a book that sat on the armrest of a puffy chair as if it could slather the front with jam.

Ophelia squared her jaw. "Not today," she muttered. "Of all the things to go wrong…" They'd been having such a peaceful afternoon until this happened.

How *had* this happened? She hadn't taken a good look at the potions on the counter to rule them out as a cause. Maybe something had spilled?

Being in sudden danger twisted a knot in her stomach she'd forgotten existed. Until she built this cozy home, the knot had waited just beneath the surface. Toxic air, marauding people, feuding factions, broken cities, and high casualty rates meant danger lurked like a beast all the time. Danger, then temporary safety—that was everyone's rhythm of life. For the first time in a long time, she cursed the civil war that had raged since the question of Danish succession generations ago.

Eyeing the doorway for roving silverware, she pressed a hand to her chest and took three deep breaths. They were safe here. They would deal with this problem and return to their books and the garden and the new tasty scones she had waiting in the warm oven.

Now, what to do? She turned her attention to the little shelves of ingredients and the cauldrons arranged along the side of the space. Only a powerful potion or spell could cause this much craziness.

She could un-magic the entire area if she had to…

It was risky—she didn't like it, but that would stop the effects of the floating, fighting utensils long enough to solve the problem. Doing so would also leave the garden and potions vulnerable. Maybe she could un-magic the cottage for only a few minutes.

Taking stock of the jars of seeds and herbs on the shelf, she chewed her lip. What was that recipe again?

A yell sounded from the other room.

Ophelia stiffened. "Everybody okay?"

"We didn't lock the shutters!" Marcellus shouted back.

Barnardo's baritone voice projected above the clanking of metal. "A knife escaped into the garden."

CHAPTER 3

spells and badgers

"Into the garden?" Ophelia rushed back into the dangerous kitchen where silverware still battled.

What must have been around half of the utensils strained from beneath the knitted blanket Barnardo gripped closed in both fists. He tilted his head toward the big kitchen window. The shutters were closed. Good thing the men had thought of shutting them. Since she always left them open, she'd only had the presence of mind to close the door. "Out there," Barnardo confirmed.

Marcellus was already at the door, ready to open it and run out after the knife.

"Make sure"—Ophelia ducked to avoid a fork—"make sure it doesn't get any of the animals. I'm going to un-magic the cottage."

Marcellus nodded grimly.

The writhing mass of metal underneath the blanket darted toward the ceiling as one. Barnardo yanked it back down. "Go quickly, Ophelia. We can handle this." Carefully, he released the blanket with one hand to snatch a spoon out of the air, which he shoved into the opening.

"I'll go as fast as I can," she said, and bolted to the library.

Why don't I keep all the spell books in the cauldron room? Of course, she hadn't considered that she might need to reverse all magic at once. The grimoire she needed sat on an upper shelf in the round room. From the ceiling hung the crocheted airship Marcellus had made for her. She'd never climbed the library ladder as quickly as she did to reach that book. Skull on the cover. That was it. She plucked it from the shelf and all but jumped the distance to the ground.

The crocheted airship plopped onto the floor next to her. She looked up. A knife hovered there, looking smug (if knives could look smug.)

"Oh...!"

She sorely wished she had time to say some choice words to that knife, but the spell needed to happen now.

"Un-magic, un-magic..." she murmured, flipping through the pages on her way to the cauldron room. From the corner of her eye, she saw the remnants of a couple pieces of sheet music littering the floor. Her heart gave a little twist.

There was the spell she needed! She bustled forward, scanning for ingredients. There weren't many. The magic needed mostly numbers, words, and gestures. "Wax and soot, twig and root..." She chose the smallest cauldron and got to work. It was hard to focus while a violent knife roamed free in her garden. *They'll be fine. They'll be fine.*

Poor Daisy! Upheaval like this would already frighten

her, and now a knife? Hopefully she'd have the presence of mind to run into her burrow.

She couldn't help remembering how close that knife in the kitchen had come to Marcellus's head too...

A commotion sounded in the kitchen beyond. She couldn't tell what they were saying. Something about "move this" and "you all right?"

Everything in her wanted to run back and check on Marcellus and Barnardo, but their best chance to stop this nonsense was this un-magicking spell in front of her. She stirred a little too quickly.

"*Thoughts black, hands apt, drugs fit, and time agreeing,*" she chanted, stirring thirteen times clockwise and seven times counterclockwise. Just to make sure the spell wouldn't cancel her magic permanently, she glanced at the tables and recipe in the grimoire. Just a few minutes. Good.

She dipped her finger into the mixture and drew a series of circles in the air.

A sensation like sparkles disappearing thrilled through her body. Could even the men feel it? Sounds and colors dulled.

Metal thudded to the floor.

With her skirt sweeping behind her, Ophelia ran to the kitchen. Polonius the badger wiggled uncomfortably on the table.

A clean table is no place for a badger, she thought with irritation before seeing why Marcellus had placed him there. His hind leg looked wrong. No blood, luckily, but the limb looked as if it had been pushed askew.

"Hold him there," Barnardo ordered Marcellus, his

shoulders lowering with relief as the silverware inside the blanket went limp.

It was oddly quiet. Then Ophelia realized it was because the potion bottles weren't murmuring to each other.

"I'll get you back to normal," she whispered to them, and then focused on Polonius.

Marcellus held the badger gently on his side. Polonius's little paws scrabbled in the air.

"What happened to him?" she asked.

"The knife knocked into him," Marcellus said with a grimace.

"Could have been worse," said Barnardo gravely. He held out the full blanket. "Is it safe to put this down?"

"Yes," Ophelia answered. "Is Polonius going to be okay?"

Barnardo eased his burden to the ground, giving a stern look to the inert silverware scattered inside. "Looks like a break in one of the joints," he said. "I can patch him up and he'll be fine."

Marcellus looked as relieved as Ophelia felt.

"Is the rest of the garden all right?" she asked.

"I captured the knife right after it did this," Marcellus explained. Polonius gave an aggravated snuffle, and Ophelia noticed a small cut to one of Marcellus's knuckles. "Nothing else in the garden was hurt. Well, it cut one of the peppers off the vine."

Barnardo sighed. He loved those peppers. "Good work."

Marcellus smiled.

"Most of the cottage is okay too, I think," said Ophelia

primly, refusing to think about the lost pages of sheet music or small things like the airship string in the library. All the living residents of the cottage came out unscathed, and that was what really mattered. "What was that? How did all the silverware start acting so crazy?"

"I figured you would know," Marcellus said, brows knitting.

Barnardo rolled up his sleeves. With great care, he cradled Polonius's bad paw in his hand. The badger snarled but didn't bite. Ophelia could all but hear him say, "Enough of this rubbish! Unhand me immediately and allow me return to my cozy den that doesn't include the likes of you foolish humans!"

"No, I don't," Ophelia confessed. She looked again at the cluster of potion bottles on the counter. One of them looked muddier than usual—brownish green with a fiery heart within. She'd never noticed it looking like that. Normally, that one (not sentient, to her knowledge) looked bottle green.

She stood and picked it up, rotating it in the light of the newly reopened garden window.

"I don't think it's the adherent," Marcellus said.

She shot him a look. Barnardo was wrapping a piece of stiff wood to Polonius's leg with a thin piece of cheesecloth. "This isn't adherent," she said. "Have you been using this as glue?"

Marcellus turned white, then red. "I... Well, I wondered why things weren't sticking. Then I remembered that the red one was an amplifier and I figured a couple drops of that would make it work better."

Ophelia set down the bottle and placed her hands on her hips. "Marcellus, what gave you the impression you could use my potions?"

"You did! You said I could learn to make potions myself if I wanted to. You said to use the adherent. I just... I didn't realize this would happen."

"I should say not!" But a small part of her warmed that he felt so comfortable around her magic—comfortable until today, at least. She exhaled. "It was an accident, I'm sure."

"I'm sorry, Ophelia."

Barnardo cleared his throat. Without looking up, he said, "I might have... used one of the potions too."

The other two gaped at him, aghast.

"You?" Ophelia exclaimed.

He stared steadfastly at Polonius's leg, tying off the wrapping. "My back hurt the other night. I couldn't sleep, and I remembered you pointing out one of the bottles earlier. I thought it was oil for the bath. Pain-relieving. I didn't use much, but I added a bit of the amplifier to that too."

"Which one?" Ophelia asked, stepping aside so he could point out the potion he meant.

When he said it was the golden one, Ophelia mentally combined what Barnardo and Marcellus had used. Together, they added wild movement and energy.

"After this bath," she said, "did you use silverware to eat anything?"

"Yes." Barnardo still didn't look at her but nodded curtly to Marcellus, who stood Polonius up on all four legs.

The badger whimpered, but then he toddled to the edge of the table. "I think he's all ready," Barnardo murmured.

Marcellus craned back at her with a tragic expression. "We shouldn't have touched the potion bottles. I'm so sorry."

Now that Polonius looked like his normal grumpy self and the three of them were out of danger, Ophelia couldn't hang onto anger. Instead, she laughed. "That was very foolish! If you wanted to use the potions, you simply had to ask. I'll show you how to make simple ones if you like. And under no circumstances are you to touch the metal-black potion."

"Spoilsport," the aforementioned potion muttered quietly.

Ophelia beamed. The potions were back.

CHAPTER 4

pirates

Polonius grumbled, but not very much, when Ophelia insisted on bundling him in the blanket that had captured the wild silverware. He made grouchy noises even as his chin nestled into the soft fabric and his eyelids lowered.

"You're lucky," Ophelia told him, carrying him out into the garden. "You had Barnardo and Marcellus to help you."

"Poppycock," she imagined him saying.

She kissed him on the head and set him down near the beehive. The kiss astonished him enough to wake up and lumber off. His leg, stiff from the splint, barely appeared to cause discomfort. Miraculous, considering he was just attacked by the butt of a knife.

Daisy's trembling nose emerged from the flower bed next to her knee. Apparently, seeing Polonius going back to normal healed not only her fear, but the hedgehog's as well.

"Glad to see he'll be all right," Barnardo said in his deep

voice as he watched her return to the cottage from the doorway.

"I am too. We had quite a scare."

"Marcellus is checking the cottage for damage."

"I expect it won't be too bad." Ophelia walked in to join Barnardo in the kitchen.

The silverware hadn't stirred since she cast the spell. Just in case, though, she planned to get rid of the mixed-up potion that had caused the whole thing and start afresh with new components so they stayed separate.

"Thank you for helping Polonius," Ophelia said. "He won't thank you, so I will."

The corners of his eyes crinkled. "No trouble at all. If anything, we caused you this trouble."

Ophelia waved her hand dismissively. "No. I mean, yes. But how many people can say they've gotten in a fight with vicious spoons?"

He chuckled. "I hope I never have to fight vicious spoons again."

"I felt like Adara the pirate."

"So did I."

Ophelia's eyebrows rose.

"After you described the story, I realized I'd read it a couple years ago." Barnardo's eyes twinkled.

At that moment, Marcellus burst into the room. "Just finished checking the main rooms. Most of the damage is fixable—lots of nicks in the walls, a couple of things ripped or sliced, one glass piece shattered."

"Which one?" Ophelia asked.

"A picture frame." One side of his mouth stretched in a sort of apologetic, froggy shrug.

"Hmm." Ophelia dusted off her hands, which didn't have much on them. She didn't ask which picture had broken. She'd find a new way to repair and mount it.

"But I think I can fix everything," Marcellus hurried to say, and revised. "Most things."

"No need to begin right now," she said, drawing them both close. The cursed silverware still lay across the floor, so her shoe caused a tangle of it to clink. She ignored it and hugged them, one in each arm. "Right now," she continued, "we need lemon scones."

Marcellus visibly relaxed. "Yes!"

They'd just had a picnic, but that felt like hours ago. After the incident with the silverware, she thought they all deserved a treat.

Barnardo began gathering forks and knives off the floor and depositing them in the sink.

"I'll teach you some magic, if you both want," she said. "Some potions work without inherent magical ability. It could be good to know what you're getting into."

Marcellus perked up. "I'd like that."

By the sink, Barnardo's face softened to a pleased smirk.

"It's settled then," said Ophelia briskly. "Magic lessons commence tomorrow."

"But right now, scones?" Marcellus asked.

"Exactly."

Ophelia piled the warm scones onto a plate that had no violent intentions, and the three of them huddled around the table to eat. She even brought out butter and honey for the occasion since they'd had such a trying day. Marcellus moaned with appreciation and Barnardo consumed four, one after the other, with mechanical precision.

Later, stuffed and satisfied, the three of them leaned back in their chairs.

"Do you think we should bring one out for Polonius?" Marcellus suggested.

"Absolutely." Ophelia snatched one off the plate and handed it to him. "Lemon scones are his favorite."

She could imagine the badger safe in his burrow, wearing a smoking jacket and luxuriating in an armchair before the fire, relieved to be home at last.

Marcellus bounded away, scone in hand, to give it to him. It was a testament to Marcellus's concern that he was willing to brave the beehive to give Polonius the treat.

"Adara the pirate, hm?" Ophelia said.

"I grew up on adventure stories," was Barnardo's only reply.

"Is that what you're always writing?"

"Adventure stories?"

"Yes."

"No. Not usually."

Ophelia's mind clung to that *not usually*, which of course meant *sometimes*. She clasped her hands in her lap to keep from demanding to see the notebook that instant.

Barnardo didn't elaborate on what other kinds of things he wrote in the little book, instead choosing to wash dishes so they'd have spoons to use for the soup later. Right now, the soup looked a mess on the stove. Ophelia wiped up the spill, shaking her head in disapproval at the naughty whisk before handing it to Barnardo.

Marcellus returned, popping quickly through the door. "I don't know if he liked it. He seemed kind of upset."

"Polonius is always a little put out," Ophelia said dismissively. "Besides, he's been through a lot today. No one expects to be pummeled by sentient knives and forks."

"I didn't know there was so much magic in the whole world," Marcellus said.

His comment made her a little sad. Marcellus was only about ten years younger than she was. Had magic disappeared that much as the conflict progressed?

Rallying, she said, "That's nothing. Want me to show you how to create apparitions that dance?" She'd concocted a shivery ghost for Halloween, and rarely used her sparklier skills, but this seemed like a good moment to pull out all the stops.

"Like, dancing ghosts?" Marcellus leaned forward.

"Or, better yet," she said, "bubbles in the shape of pirate ships."

She cast a look at Barnardo, who smiled. "I can't wait," he said.

garden swing

CHAPTER 1

carousel

Once, when Ophelia was a child, she saw a carousel. It was the old-fashioned kind with carved wooden horses, each different from all the others, painted in bold, lacquered streaks of white, red, black, blue, and yellow. Some had their mouths open as if in fright. Others bore themselves proudly, necks high. Still others had all four legs outstretched in opposite directions, frozen in a dead sprint. One had a black bridle and an ornate gold and red saddle. That was her favorite.

Although she learned later that carousels usually played music and spun round and round, this one dipped slightly where the ground had given way under one side. It didn't move. The plastic circus-tent canopy cast a shadow over several of the straining horses. But Ophelia still thought the carousel was beautiful.

She hadn't considered that memory for a long time. She dipped into the past as some people dipped into spiked punch—cautiously and only on certain occasions. Remembering the white-bright ground around the carousel as her parents hustled her past it to shelter didn't stir up happy thoughts. The horses, though, and the mechanical apparatus they pranced on, constructed only to make children laugh, created a glow in the center of an otherwise gloomy moment.

"So... what do you think?" Marcellus held down the large sheet of paper on the island in the center of the kitchen. He eyed her hesitantly.

She blinked a couple times, trying to clear her head. One of the potions on the counter near the sink murmured, "What's on that paper? Can you see?"

"No, I can't *see*," replied the metal-black potion, who was almost always in a bad mood.

Marcellus seemed to take Ophelia's pause as a negative comment on his work. "If it'll take up too much room in the garden, I totally understand. Maybe it's a bad idea."

Ophelia set a hand over his to stop him from rolling up his hand-drawn plans. On the top half of the paper, he'd drawn a map of the cottage and garden, complete with the location of every tree, beehive, and animal home. On the bottom, he'd sketched out what looked like a train track to run around the area, except that sometimes the track crossed over itself. One glance had told her she'd misread the map. That couldn't be an ordinary train.

For one, Marcellus was a clever mechanic. He wouldn't make a disaster of twisted tracks. Second, the car he'd drawn to ride the track didn't look like a train engine at all. It looked like a horse. This wasn't a train track. It was a plan for a small rollercoaster.

"It's not a bad idea," she said, though privately she thought this plan did cover far too much of her garden. "I love the idea of installing something purely for fun. Maybe not something that needs so much metal."

Marcellus tipped his mouth at that. It was true. Even with her creativity at reusing resources and his skill at putting the pieces together until they worked, it would take months to gather enough pieces to make a rollercoaster. Besides, she didn't like the idea of one of them—Ophelia, Marcellus, or Barnardo—suiting up in her makeshift anti-toxin gear over and over again to search.

"You're right," he said. "Even if we dismantle the pumpkin trellis and use wood, that won't be enough. I just..." He faded to silence, evidently looking for words.

Perhaps he had memories similar to hers. "Do you like rollercoasters?" she asked.

He met her eyes. "I've never ridden one. I asked Barnardo, and *he* has, but you know how he is. He didn't seem to enjoy it."

Ophelia laughed. "We do need a little excitement." Lately, her memories had been resurfacing like bubbles in a boiling brew. She needed a project. "Why does your roller-coaster vehicle look like a horse?"

Marcellus perked up at the question. "I was trying to plan for materials we might actually be able to find. Near our crash site, I'm pretty sure I saw a wooden horse, like a rocking horse, and I thought it would make good decoration, or materials, at least."

"You left it there?" Survivors had probably taken it by now. She tried to imagine passing something so interesting and not picking it up to bring back to her charmed bunker.

Years ago, when she still went on expeditions outside, she'd scavenged everything of interest within a couple days' walk of her bunker. Even curiosities she wasn't sure she'd want came home with her. That was the thing about wastelands—you couldn't let anything more go to waste. That was how she found Polonius the badger, a framed picture of real butterflies, a tin whistle, and a mixing bowl shaped like a sunflower, among many other oddments and friends that eventually built her lopsided, lovely home.

"It might still be there," said Marcellus. He obviously hadn't developed her dragon-like urgency for hoarding treasure. Maybe that was all for the best.

Ophelia's mind whirled. Barnardo had returned to the crash site once to pick up a tiny gear, but he hadn't brought back anything else. Ophelia's mind at the time had been full of preparations for Barnardo's secret birthday party, so she hadn't the sense to be bothered. Now, thinking of all the prizes that could still be out there, her mind stretched out again beyond the cozy *here* of home. It was the stretching that was dangerous, when no immediate need called for it.

Instinctively, she glanced around the kitchen and into the tunnel-like hallway beyond. Through the kitchen window on the opposite side of the room, she spotted Daisy the hedgehog trundling up the garden path with Bird hopping at her side.

Harumph! she told herself. It was foolish to be afraid of every little thing. Adventures were not born without taking risks.

"Perhaps," she mused, looking again at Marcellus's drawing, "we could make something a little smaller."

Digging out a pen from the drawer, she circled a spot and told Marcellus her idea.

His pale face lifted into an enormous, crinkled smile. "That'd be perfect!"

CHAPTER 2

swing

Barnardo, a dubious expression covering his craggy face, handed the ladder to Marcellus. Bird flittered around Barnardo's shoulders, but Ophelia couldn't tell if the motion was meant to warn, encourage, or simply relish the fact that Barnardo was there.

Ophelia oversaw the exchange with hardly more confidence than Barnardo seemed to have. They shared a swift look. Perhaps there was a better way to do this.

With a low scraping noise and a mighty heave, Marcellus dragged the long ladder onto the big square generator with him. "I think I have it!" he declared.

"Hm," was all Barnardo said in answer. He didn't let go of the ladder.

"I've never tried to reach the ceiling before," Ophelia confessed.

"Why should you?" Barnardo adjusted his hold on the end rung while Marcellus wrestled with the contraption on his end.

"I never had a reason before."

"The bats," Marcellus reminded them. It was true. On Halloween, two bats named Bubble and Trouble had snuck in through a fault in the ceiling. Considering the toxic air outside, it really would be best to patch that up. Her magic could stave off the worst of the effects, but that level of effort would negatively affect her garden, which already required a steady stream of care.

"Hm," Barnardo said again. "While you're up there, see if you can find the hole."

Marcellus nodded, pulling the extendable ladder further up.

Barnardo finally released his hold.

Marcellus, already sweaty with effort, crouched, his fist tight on the rungs. Ophelia had only used the ladder to construct the cottage roof and string the lights above the garden path. Oh, and she'd dragged it out once more to paint the interior wall of the Inner Box to look like an enchanted forest disappearing into the distance. It made the entire space feel bigger.

"Think it'll reach?" asked Barnardo. His voice had taken on the cadence of someone used to leading others and solving problems.

Marcellus craned to look up. The ceiling disappeared in dimness, ornamented with faintly glowing blue bioluminescence. "Not sure."

Barnardo looked at Ophelia. "Do you know the measurements of the inner and outer bunkers?"

She fixed him with a glance saying he should know better than to ask. Just last week she'd expanded the garden with one of the potions murmuring on the counter. "What do you think?"

A warm smile thawed his face. "No."

"No," she confirmed. "Measurements don't stay in place."

"Because of you, I'd wager."

She didn't deny it. Instead, she tucked a strand of hair behind her ear in a particularly impish way.

"Ophelia," Marcellus called down, "is there a way to get me up there if the ladder isn't long enough?"

She still wasn't used to this new level of trust he had in her magic. He trusted her, of course, but to suggest magic as a solution was a recent development. She thought of the brew that had made Daisy float above the cauldron. Doubtful it would work on humans, and it was dangerous to try. Still, the mental image of Marcellus hovering in midair, flailing his long limbs, trying to swim toward the ceiling, made her stifle a laugh.

"No, nothing I have ready," she answered.

"Well, I think I have enough to get on with up here," Marcellus said, straightening again and gauging the distance to the top of the bunker before looking down at the coil of rope at his feet. "Why don't you start on the chair part? I can get this done."

It was nice seeing Marcellus and Barnardo in their element. Marcellus had that burning, purposeful look he got when he was fixing something.

Too late, she remembered the little bottle she used to help her lift heavy things. She could have offered it to Marcellus.

"Come down and put on the suit before you climb," Ophelia insisted. *The suit* was the puffy beekeeping ensemble. She knew Marcellus hated it, but it would cushion a fall if the ladder was in fact too short to reach the ceiling.

"I'll be fine."

"Marcellus."

Barnardo raised his eyebrows. Both he and Marcellus knew that when she used that tone, she wouldn't be contradicted.

"I need to be free to move," Marcellus countered, climbing down.

"Then leave the gloves."

His face half-scrunched with annoyance, but he nodded and walked past them toward the cottage.

"He'll be fine," Barnardo said. "The chair—do you have materials already?" He fixed Ophelia with one of his long stares, as if he'd known her far longer than a few months and could therefore guess exactly what she was thinking.

"Probably." She hadn't forgotten the broken carousel, the only carnival ride she'd ever seen in person. Part of her wished she could find it again and repair it. She'd given new life to other objects. What fun would it be for one of those carousel horses to fly through the air instead of a simple chair? She didn't know if a swing counted as a ride, but, since the cables would be mounted to the ceiling, she thought it should. The horses were lost now. Best not to consider them.

"I have options," she went on, leading the way back into the cottage.

Polonius the badger waddled across their path, casting

her a shrewd look. If he had his way, she thought, everything would be utterly practical, with reading and mince pies and armchairs in front of the fire the only luxuries allowed. He disappeared into the foliage.

Ophelia and Barnardo strode together into the cottage, knocking soil off their boots as they entered. "The ladder in the library could be broken and repurposed as a chair. I have plenty of blankets to serve as cushions."

Barnardo flattened his lips. Clearly, he didn't like that idea. She wasn't exceptionally fond of it either. Who didn't want a ladder in their library?

"Or," she said, "we could simply use some of the blankets, like a hammock."

His eyebrows did a tricky, curling thing that meant he didn't like the idea but didn't want to tell her so.

She put her hands on her hips. "Our resources are somewhat limited, you know." She had no desire to dismantle the cottage, but she'd sacrifice a piece for some new enjoyment.

"I know, I know," he said, low.

"Do you really think the airship is gone?" The question left her before she could stuff it back in her mouth.

Barnardo grew serious. "Most of it. Probably."

"You think it's not worth looking?"

"I said *probably*." Ice glittered in his eyes, not unkindly. With a sigh, he straightened and looked like the military man he was. The wristwatch shone, freshly polished, on his wrist. "The ladder, the fabric... They're good ideas, but for one person. Don't you think the swing should be bigger?"

"For all three of us? Of course!" she exclaimed, frowning. "But where—"

At that moment, Marcellus emerged from his room, clad in puffy pink robes and beekeeping regalia. His expression was sour.

"Beautiful," Ophelia declared.

"Competent," Barnardo put in.

"Off to get the job done." Marcellus turned away, taking wide, careful steps. He snagged a bramble pasty off a plate on his way out, as if it were some kind of payment.

Ophelia and Barnardo looked at each other and laughed behind their hands.

CHAPTER 3

gear

Seeing Marcellus in full gear unlocked something inside Ophelia. It was as if she were a clock whose mechanisms needed a subtle push to make everything move in unison.

Even if the crashed airship had been scavenged for parts, the remaining shell could still prove useful for more than just the swing.

She whirled on Barnardo. "We need to get to that airship." When Barnardo looked doubtful, she repeated, "Yes, we."

Shuffling back into the kitchen in a flurry of speed, she faced the chaotic assembly of potion bottles. "What do I need?" she muttered, clinking around to find the ones she needed. Amplifier, heavy objects, metal-black for protection... Where was it? There! In the back, beside the shy, square bottle, was a small round one made of cloudy glass. It was inert, without a discernable personality, like so many of the others had. It had been so long since she'd used it that she'd all but forgotten about its existence. "Home!" she said, holding the tiny bottle aloft with the others.

Barnardo came up beside her. "What are these for?"

She set down the little cloudy potion. "Finding home again."

A larger jar. "Clearing out the toxin."

Next came the metal-black potion. "Protection."

("Finally!" muttered the metal-black potion darkly. "Do I get to kill someone?")

She set the clear blue amplifier down next. "Extra magic."

The amplifier sparkled proudly, but the metal-black potion seemed to take her description as a slight and said something cruel. Ophelia saw more dandelions and songs in her future to pacify the fickle amplifying potion.

"Sounds useful," said Barnardo, ignoring the emotional exchange between the blue and black potions.

"I haven't gone out in far too long," said Ophelia, sweeping the four bottles into one of her deep pockets. The rest of the potions still sitting on the counter gave a collective protest, as if they'd just witnessed an unfair point being given to the opposing team in a sporting match.

"Because we have this place," Barnardo commented.

Her heart warmed at his repetition of *we*. Barnardo and Marcellus saw her cozy cottage and garden as their home too.

"Yes," she replied crisply. "But what is life without occasional adventure? It makes coming home all the better." The very thought made her long for her armchair and blankets and books and tea. A familiar longing, but welcome.

"Should we tell Marcellus?"

Ophelia glanced at the clock ticking away on the wall. It said it was eleven fifty-three in the morning. She remembered the wastes not getting especially dangerous (minus the toxic air and pervasive violence among survivors) until after eight fifteen each evening. This time of year, eight fifteen was full dark. That should give them enough time to go there and back again, wouldn't it?

"Yes. Let me get the gear." She fished out the amplifier and handed it to Barnardo. "Sing to this." At Barnardo's astonishment—the bottle looked particularly fragile in his big hand—she clarified, "It needs songs to work, and I'm getting our outfits together."

As if in answer, the amplifier shimmered with anticipation.

"Any song, or...?"

Ophelia had seen Barnardo confused before, but the panic gleaming in his eyes seemed to say that he'd never faced a foe so formidable as *singing*.

"Any song. Have you heard 'Doubt Thou the Stars are Fire'?" It was a popular Liegeman song. Ophelia herself subscribed to no side in the ongoing conflict, but she knew the tune well.

Barnardo nodded solemnly.

There was an awkward pause.

"He's not doing anything," murmured the amplifier.

"Hush," Ophelia told it. "*Doubt thou the stars are fire,*" she prompted.

"*Doubt that the sun doth move.*" Barnardo's voice grew

creaky and uncertain as he tried to sing, but he carried the tune well enough to recognize.

Ophelia gestured for him to continue while she rushed off to prepare gear for two people to go on an adventure. "Gear" constituted the gray sweater Marcellus had crocheted for Barnardo with a large letter B on it, the old-timey scuba helmet, two fluffy robes, a pair of oven mitts, a breathing tube, heavy boots, goggles, a long scarf, and a rusty wagon she kept near the big generator.

Barnardo's singing gained steam and filtered through the windows into the garden. He still barely kept the tune, but the song had the endearing quality that develops when one believes they won't be overheard, a sincerity.

Ophelia smiled and grasped the handle of the wagon languishing amid a patch of rogue hollyhocks.

"What do you have there?" Marcellus called from above.

Ophelia looked up. Marcellus stood atop the generator box, securing the bottom of the ladder. The ladder, fully extended, reached almost out of sight. She didn't care for the view. It made her dizzy, for one. For another, she preferred to think that the ceiling of her hideaway reached an interminable distance, rather than being accessible by ladder. It was foolish, maybe, and impractical, but she didn't care. It was lovely to feel that one had *space*.

"A wagon," she replied. "Barnardo and I are going on an expedition."

"An expedition outside?" Marcellus cocked his head. The mesh on the beekeeper's hat swooshed gently to one side.

"We'll be careful, and no doubt gone for only a few hours. Take care of Daisy and Bird and the rest for me." She dragged the red wagon out from among the flowers. The wheel snagged on a tough stem.

"Don't we have materials for a chair here?" he asked, jumping down and taking off the hat. His face shone with sweat, and a lock of hair stuck to his temple.

"Not what we need. Plus, with more people living here, it's good to get new supplies now and then." With a hard pull, she freed the wagon and rolled it onto the path.

"I could help."

Ophelia halted. "No. You're helping here." She couldn't have said why she didn't want him to come. Something about concern, but she and Barnardo would be fine. It wasn't as if Marcellus was a child, but *someone* had to stay behind at the cottage to keep it ready for them. Why not him?

Looking up at his earnest face, she relented a little. "I don't have enough protection for another person. And it's dangerous."

Marcellus opened his mouth.

"I'm a witch. I'll be fine."

He closed his mouth again. Then his eyes slid out of focus as he concentrated on something else. "Is that... singing?"

Ophelia burst out laughing. "Barnardo's singing to the amplifier. Want to join him? I'm sure the potion would be delighted!"

Horror crossed Marcellus's features, and he shook his

head vigorously. He'd seen her entertain that potion many times to coax it into behaving.

"Are you sure?" she couldn't help adding.

"Yes. No. I almost have the ladder ready." He all but sprinted the few steps back to it as fast as the fluffy pink robe would allow.

"Wonderful. Barnardo and I will be off shortly. We'll return before sundown, hopefully with a swing and a few more oddments."

"Want to take the hat?" he offered.

She paused a moment. A mere hat wouldn't do much to protect Marcellus if he were to fall, but the additional barrier could give her or Barnardo a few more toxin-free seconds. "Yes. Hand it down."

He obeyed, and she plunked it into the wagon with the rest of the gear before pulling it back into the cottage.

On her way in, Polonius's stripey face poked out from beneath some greenery. His black bead eyes regarded her. She could have sworn that look meant, "Be careful out there, my dear Ophelia."

And she would respond over Barnardo's faint chorus, "Of course I will, my dear sir."

CHAPTER 4

outside/inside

Ophelia and Barnardo faced the heavy exterior door. On their way out of the cottage, covered in makeshift protective gear, she had removed the breathing tube from her mouth and quoted a spell to the potion that allowed her to move heavy things. Then she counted to thirteen. She poured a drop on the deadbolt. Still, she hesitated to pull it to.

Barnardo caught her eye, a heartening twinkle in it.

With a deep breath, Ophelia replaced the breathing tube, adjusted her goggles, and heaved the bolt to the side. White light poured through the opening into the barren inner perimeter of the huge bunker. The air itself smelled familiar and electric. She sneezed before plowing forward. The determination that had fueled her to build her cozy home kicked in again and a small excitement bubbled behind her sternum. Even though the landscape stretched into a blur of white and tan, bleached of all life, adventure called, and Ophelia's lips twitched into a smile.

"It's just this way," came Barnardo's voice, muffled behind the round scuba helmet. He pointed a gloved hand forward. His other hand gripped the handle of the red wagon.

The land rose into lumps of sandy hills. There, on the right, Ophelia had found the book of seasons. Out there, far on the left, she'd discovered the glass cloche that now covered the stuffed Elf Owl. Two days out, straight ahead, she'd stumbled across an abandoned building, its roof gone, where she'd gathered piles of sheet music, plywood, loose fabric, a box full of small gears and wires, and two kinds of seeds.

Ophelia owned this landscape as much as anyone else. This world was hers. She let the knowledge seep in and found a kind of strength in it.

She and Barnardo trundled forward. Barnardo's puffy form created half-moon indentations in the sand. Here and there, as they walked, the detritus of military excursions littered the ground, breaking up the monotony. She'd already investigated most of those pieces of twisted metal. What she thought she could use, she'd already brought back to improve her cottage.

Secretly, of course, Ophelia wanted to locate the wooden horse that Marcellus had described. She didn't have much hope of finding it, but the image of a carved horse tipped over in the sand-strewn wasteland made her itch to retrieve it and give it new life in her garden.

Because of the layers of clothes and masks they wore, Barnardo and Ophelia didn't speak much. Barnardo's ice-blue eyes scanned the horizon with his trademark seriousness, but this time, he also looked wary. Roving bands sometimes crisscrossed this area. It had been ages since Ophelia had heard them pass outside. That could partially have been due to the constant hum of the generator and the double walls separating her oasis from the outside world.

Wind whipped around Ophelia's ears, covered with the beekeeper's helmet. The hot-cold of the toxic air threatened at the gaps of her clothing. It wasn't a new sensation, but it did make her want to swath her entire body in thick blankets while she lit a candle, sipped some tea, and read a book. Perhaps while Daisy the hedgehog slept nearby.

Adventure was a tricky thing. It made the blood burn with courage, which was good. It also made coming home a joy, which was better.

Barnardo glanced at the sky. The movement looked awkward with the crazy ensemble he wore. Hers wasn't any better. The sun burned white through the white haze of sky. They were traveling roughly south.

Where in all this waste, Ophelia wondered, was that carousel she'd seen as a girl? Nothing they passed looked remotely like the carousel or the horse Marcellus claimed to have seen.

Hours passed until the sun tipped past them, slanting their shadows the other way. Ophelia's face chafed from the goggles and her feet chafed from all that walking.

"When will the marauders come?" muttered the metal-black potion from within her pocket. "Let me at them!"

"We're alone out here," she whispered back. The high, thin breath of air through the tube was hardly audible.

"I finally get a chance to have some fun, and I'm stuck doing nothing with these..."

"Shh!"

Another bottle in her pocket gasped at the metal-black potion's language.

Ophelia tuned them out and kept walking. Barnardo seemed not to have heard them.

Finally, a large shape bubbled into view.

An airship. A Liegeman airship, complete with its symbol of the sun on the balloon envelope. Ophelia wrinkled her nose, but her heart sped up with the discovery too.

"That's it?" she asked, carefully enunciating each syllable.

Barnardo nodded, eyes alight through the grimy glass of the helmet.

The main balloon part hung ragged and torn. The gondola lay on its side. Two walls of the basket were gone. Scorch marks blackened the inner workings of the machine, but more remained than Ophelia would have guessed.

She understood why Barnardo hadn't taken other pieces back to the cottage the last time he'd visited the wreck. It was a miracle that Marcellus and Barnardo had survived the crash at all. The thought pierced her with the blade-strength of love. Thank goodness they had.

Ophelia cleared her throat and bustled forward, inspecting the crashed airship for anything that could serve as a seat for the swing. Barnardo parked the wagon beside the bulk of the debris. The fluttering remains of fabric cast the wreck in shadow. Shadow out here still burned more brightly than her softly lit bunker, though, and her eyes tired of it.

After a couple minutes, she sucked in a breath, removed the tube, and asked, "See anything?"

Barnardo lifted part of the burned engine with his gloved hand, then set it back down. "Not yet."

She scanned one more time for the fabled horse. It must have been taken long ago.

That's perfectly fine, she told herself.

She rounded the gondola, which was only large enough for maybe four people to stand comfortably, to inspect the other side.

Partially submerged in the sand lay a broken chunk of the huge basket. It had two sides welded together at a ninety-degree angle. Ophelia approached, judging her own size against the wood and metal piece. Could three of them sit side by side?

It was a perfect fit.

"Barnardo!" she called.

"Did you find something?" he asked, rounding the corner.

She pointed at the chunk of debris and smiled.

"That'll do nicely," he agreed.

Together, they hefted it to perch on the wagon.

With the seat safely ready to be transported back to the bunker, Ophelia asked the fun, superfluous question: "Marcellus said something about a horse near here? A carousel or a rocking horse? Did you see something like that?"

He shook his head. "No. Did you want to find it?"

"I did. But we don't need to spend more time out here. We have what we came for."

"Best to go back soon."

"Absolutely." Ophelia wasn't filled with regret, but she did feel a slight pang.

"Do you like carousel horses?" Barnardo asked as he continued to dig through the wreckage. He sounded very far away.

"Of course," she replied, snappish.

"Never rode a carousel," he said. "I rode a rollercoaster once. Terrible."

Ophelia burst out in a brittle laugh. "No rollercoasters for me."

"Trust me. You're not missing anything."

Ophelia thought Marcellus would disagree, and she would dearly love to try a rollercoaster herself, but she only raised her eyebrows in answer. He probably couldn't see over all the layers of clothes and goggles and bushy hair. So she said, "I think a swing is just right for us."

CHAPTER 5

together

Ophelia heaved a long sigh of relief when she and Barnardo finally returned home and closed the door behind them. The wagon rattled over the concrete floor to the Inner Box where her world awaited. She put the breathing tube away immediately.

Along the way, they'd picked up the large metal piece to serve as a sort of bench for the swing, a pair of scraggly yellow flowers that needed a home, and an assortment of bits and pieces salvaged from the wreck. Their most surprising find wasn't a wooden horse (they never found one) but three small pots of paint and a brush tucked away in a corner, the paints still fresh. Barnardo's cheek crinkled when he saw it. They promptly set it all in the wagon. Thank goodness she'd thought to bring the amplifier to enhance her revelation spell or else they wouldn't have made that discovery.

Ophelia stuffed the cloudy home-finding bottle deep in her pocket. She never felt truly lost, but it was a relief for the potion to tug them gently in the right direction to confirm they hadn't gotten turned around. The wasteland could shift at odd times, after all.

When she'd found Polonius as a cub, sniffing around a little patch of ground poky with dried grass, like a barren island among the sand, she'd scooped him up and *whoosh!* A strong wind blew grains of sand into her eyes and covered the grass. Hills slanted different directions. After hours of wandering to find her bunker again, she'd finally resolved to dig a shelter in a shallow dune for the night. As soon as she crawled in, she laughed. All that time spent being grumpy, holding a grumpy badger in her arms, and the solution was right on the tip of her tongue.

"The selfsame sun that shines upon this court
Hides not his visage from our cottage but
Looks on alike. Will't please you, sir, be gone?"

Polonius had looked at her with as much sarcasm as an animal could muster. She loved him dreadfully.

The next morning, when she peeked out from their hiding place, a star sparked in her vision, like the white spots that moved when one was faint. And that was enough to guide her home. Since then, she never left without a batch of that distilled spell.

Barnardo opened the door for her to rumble through. Green seeped back into her nose, her eyes, and the slivers of exposed skin (which felt feverish and had to be scrubbed right away). Beside her, Barnardo heaved a quiet sigh.

Marcellus saw them from atop the generator as they made their way down the garden path under strings of lights. He waved his whole arm. "Hey!" He jumped down and trotted toward them. He wasn't wearing the fluffy robe anymore. "Everything okay? Did you get it?"

Ophelia rattled the wagon's handle. "Of course we did. That and more."

They reached the threshold of the cottage with its shingles and sloping roof and improbable rooms. The walls bowed out just a little, as if they couldn't contain all the coziness inside. Ophelia longed for a bath and a blanket.

"Absolutely no action at all," muttered the metal-black potion as she clinked it onto the shelf with the others in the kitchen. It swirled dangerously.

"I'll let you loose on some weeds later," she promised.

A grim and happy sparkle showed that would do.

Through the window, she could see Barnardo unloading the wagon, still with his helmet on.

"Let Marcellus do that," she called. "Get in here and get clean."

Bird, who had been swooping joyfully around Barnardo's head, tweeting loudly, flew off in disappointment as he obeyed and followed her into the cottage. Clanks and grunts meant Marcellus was dealing with the large seat for the chair.

"You go first," she said, drawing off the beekeeper's hat and goggles. "I'll keep the magic waiting." She meant the cleansing spell that had revived the men the first time they stumbled into her world.

"I can wait," he answered, steady but slightly absurd in his helmet.

"No such thing. Go!"

He cast her a look that said he *could* argue but chose not to. Then he nodded and headed off for a bath.

Still wearing her gloves, she put a kettle on. Mint and bramble tea was in order.

"Ophelia."

She turned to find Marcellus in the doorway. He'd pushed his sleeves past his elbows and his hands were grimy with dirt and grease.

"It's all unloaded. Do you want me to put it all somewhere...?"

"Don't worry about that for now." She liked organizing things herself. Well, *organizing* was a strong word. *Placing* was probably better. Having thirty-two new screws and nuts and bolts and strips of adhesive made her insides light.

Marcellus smiled, big and honest. "All right. I got the ropes to stick. Did you see?"

She was ashamed to say she hadn't. She'd barely looked up at all, except to acknowledge Marcellus waving at them.

"Oh. Well, they're solid. Not going anywhere." His expressive face quirked.

Ophelia smiled. The sound of water boiling in the kettle grew deeper. It was almost ready. "Thank you."

"I'm glad you're both safe."

The metal-black potion huffed.

Ophelia did too. "Why wouldn't we be?" But they both remembered the time when Barnardo had gone out alone and they had worried. She hurried on. "That seat will need cushions, of course. It has too many sharp edges to be comfortable."

"Do you have some ready?"

"Please," she chided.

The kettle whistled and she poured three cups, one for each of them.

Shortly, Barnardo emerged, damp and dressed in new clothes. She performed the spell to banish any lingering effects from the toxin that might prey on his bones, then she drew another bath and got in. The hot water felt lovely. Candles lit the space, and she brought a book and a cup of tea with her. Bubbles and scented soaps filled the air. Each moment that passed soaked the tension from her shoulders.

Bathed and swathed in her fluffiest remaining outfit— she probably looked like Daisy when she tucked herself into a ball, perfectly round—Ophelia emerged. The men were munching on poppyseed scones and bramble pasties. She quickly spelled herself and joined them.

Marcellus spoke excitedly about the mechanics of attaching the seat. Barnardo, still with a hint of the toxin-gray around his eyes, listened attentively. Together, they came up with a plan. Marcellus would drill new holes in the metal through which the ropes would run, Ophelia would assist with the floating potion she had accidentally made some days before, Barnardo would help muscle the wide seat into place. Add cushions and voila! A swing with a view of the entire garden.

Several scones and one cup of tea later, all three set to work. With the help of the amplifier (which still glowed happy from Barnardo's song), Ophelia recreated the floating mixture and found long cushions and patchy throw blankets while Marcellus and Barnardo worked outside. Daisy the hedgehog squeaked in terror when

Ophelia accidentally upended her from nesting in the folds of a blanket.

"This is why I don't always invite you inside," Ophelia murmured, watching Daisy scurry underneath the bed. Poor thing.

Prepared with potion and cushions bundled in her arms, Ophelia waddled out into the garden.

"One, two, three!" cried Barnardo's sonorous voice.

Ophelia rounded the corner to find them both atop the generator, struggling to lift the seat so the rope met the holes in the metal. Ophelia flung the blankets down on some dry ferns and wielded the floating potion. It hadn't needed rhyme or meter before in order to work, so she simply dabbed some in her palm and held it outstretched toward the pair of men.

They stopped straining, muscles softening. Their eyes widened and brows furrowed. Finally, they let go of the chair altogether except to guide it into place and secure the fastenings.

Marcellus turned a wild smile on Ophelia. "That's wonderful!"

She grinned, bundling up the blankets in her arms once more to hand them up to Barnardo, who took them. The wagon and the other pieces taken from the wreckage parked neatly beside the industrial green box. She scrambled on top of the generator with them. From here, she could see most of the garden, from the apple tree to the beehive to the beds of thyme, the decorative mushroom she'd made, the path, the lights, Gertrude the rabbit and Polonius the badger gazing up at them with furtive and unsure expressions...

Barnardo somewhat awkwardly arranged pillows and blankets on the seat, which hung far enough to the side of the generator that they could swing over plants rather than the green eyesore.

Ophelia checked to make sure the arrangement was cozy enough and stopped.

Painted in bright shades of yellow, green, and blue on the back of the seat was a carousel horse. It wasn't a masterpiece by any means. The nose wasn't long enough and the legs were uneven, but she recognized the shape immediately. The tang of paint sharpened the air when she stood behind the swing. She touched the design delicately with a finger. Yellow coated her fingertip.

"Don't touch that," said Barnardo. "It's not dry."

"Did you do this?" she asked.

"We thought it would... We thought you'd like it." The slight sheepishness in his tone only warmed her heart more.

"Do you? What do you think?" Marcellus asked. "I came up with the idea and Barnardo painted it."

Sharpness bit at her eyes. "Good," she answered brusquely. "It's good."

"Let's dry it out, then," Barnardo said, equally short.

First he, then Ophelia, then Marcellus climbed onto the long seat. It didn't have armrests or handholds besides the rope. Marcellus and Barnardo hung on, and Ophelia grasped both of their hands in hers. Together, they pumped their legs. Ophelia's stomach pitched as they floated back and forth, higher and higher. The ropes were long, so they could go as high as they wanted if they were careful.

Below them, Polonius and Daisy and Gertrude

watched. Bird and the bats, Bubble and Trouble, flew around them in confused excitement. The ground looked green and living. The pumpkin trellis missed their feet by inches. The scent of apples and rosemary swept past them. Wind dried their cheeks and eyes.

Soon, they were all laughing. Ophelia's chest filled with so much joy it ached. Flying like this above the world she'd made, gripping Marcellus and Barnardo's hands tight, felt a lot like magic.

And she should know.

acknowledgments

This little book would never have seen the light except for C.H. Lyn, another multi-genre author and champion of indie writers who believed in this story. She gave me the encouragement I needed to expand on the "Power to Charm" world.

Obviously, my love of Shakespeare's *Hamlet* played a role too. I wrote this mashup of cozy, post-apocalyptic, witchy fantasy just for myself, so I threw *Hamlet* references in there. (Cut to all my friends, family, and co-workers nodding their heads without surprise.)

"Charm," which I originally pictured in a Shakespeare-inspired short story collection, took on a life of its own. I love spending time with Ophelia, Barnardo, Marcellus, Daisy, Polonius, and the rest. In a world that often feels chaotic, everyone needs a safe place to rest sometimes. For me, Ophelia's home became that. I hope you find it to be a place of comfort too.

also by carly stevens

Tanyuin Academy series (YA fantasy)

Firian Rising

Into the Unreal

Kingdoms on Fire

Tanyuin Academy Stories (short story collection)

Dark academia

Laertes: A Hamlet Retelling

The Hamlet Reader (compilation of *Hamlet* research)

* * *

Find more about Carly Stevens' work, including bonus stories, at
https://carly-stevens.com